Shadows Of The Seen

A Novel

Timothy Gager

"Guns don't kill people, people kill people." However, as Timothy Gager's nasty little parable demonstrates, the people who kill people are the very people who should not have access to firearms. In case you've been living under a rock and the national carnage has escaped your notice, it's just too easy for a lunatic to get a gun.

Gregory Gibson, author of *Gone Boy* and other books

"Timothy Gager weaves a narrative story that is entertaining and addresses the gun crisis in our country. Politicians, lobbyists, and our mental health system are shown to need a cleansing in Gager's most recent work."

Barbara Legere, author of *Keven's Choice*, and *Talk to Me, I'm Grieving*

"Timothy Gager is a writer who has written about gun violence as it needs to be written. He goes past the quick "post" or "reel" that we see after each shooting that we hear about in the news. We get the sound, the smell, the feel of what gun violence leaves behind. Sometimes, it hurts to read his words, but then again, it hurts to be the victim of gun violence, so get over it and read on. We can't imagine the pain, but Timothy can. "Big men, big guns, big egos to fill, they don't even need a reason, got a license to kill…" from my song "Standing Your Ground"

Kemp Harris, Songwriter, Actor and Storyteller

Copyright © 2025 • All Rights Reserved
Timothy Gager
Pierian Springs Press

Other than review quotes or academic excerpts,
no part of this work may be reproduced
without explicit permission.

First Edition, May 2025
Library of Congress Control Number: *pending*
ISBN 978-1-965784-09-9 Hardback
ISBN 978-1-965784-10-5 Paperback

Cover Graphic Design & Book Typography by Kurt Lovelace.
Cover artwork by Pierian Springs Press
Cover type *Bauhaus Dessau* **Alfarn** by Céline Hurka,
Elia Preuss, Flavia Zimbardi,
Hidetaka Yamasaki, and Luca Pellegrini.
Chapter titles in **Jenson** by Robert Slimbach.
Chapter titles in **Baskerville**; Body text set in **Nimbus**.
Chapter dropcaps set in **Mrs Eaves XL**
by Emigre Foundry designer Zuzana Licko.
Flourishes set in Emigre Foundry **Dalliance** by Frank Heine.
Emigre Foundry **ZeitGuys** by Bob Aufuldish, Eric Donelan.
Typefaces licensed Adobe, Linotype, Emigre, & URW GmbH.

Pierian Springs Press

PSPress.Pub
Pierian Springs Press, Inc
30 N Gould St, Ste 25398
Sheridan, Wyoming 82801-6317

In Gratitude

To all of those touched by any of the subject matter of this book, and for those looking for solutions.

For the support of the fellowship and the personal support I received from Chris F., Sheila S., Jenna E, Jenn N., J.D., Kevin, Smokin' Al and my friends at Happy Hour at a time when I most needed it.

Always to my siblings, Martha, Mary, and Fred, my children Gabe, daughter-in-law Brie and daughter Caroline.

Contents

Foreword
Seamus McGraw

Prologue

Section 1, Part I
Candace

Chapter 1: The Nicene Creed 7
Chapter 2: The Politics of Men 15
Chapter 3: Votes 23
Chapter 4: Yes, Governor 27
Chapter 5: Take the Money and Run 31
Chapter 6: Enemies 35
Chapter 7: Face-Off 39

Section 1, Part II
Peter

Chapter 1: Backward 45
Chapter 2: Hush Money 49
Chapter 3: They're In The Trees 51
Chapter 4: More on the Blackout Tunnel 59
Chapter 5: Therapissed 61
Chapter 6: Only If You Want It 67
Chapter 7: Rage, Fury, Wrath, and Irritation 71

Section 1, Part III

Lucky

Chapter 1: Prayers or Just Lucky 77
Chapter 2: I Do 85
Chapter 3: Ward Cleaver, I'm Not 91
Chapter 4: The Anniversary 95
Chapter 5: The Turning Point 99
Chapter 6: Lucky? 103
Chapter 7: Bingo 109
Chapter 8: Home Game 115
Chapter 9: Sump Pump 121
Chapter 10: Moving 123

Section 2, Part I

Candace

Chapter 1: Shootings 127
Chapter 2: Dreams 131
Chapter 3: Conflict 133
Chapter 4: How To Resolve Conflict 137
Chapter 5: How People Can Change 141
Chapter 6: The Reveal 145
Chapter 7: Tightrope 149
Chapter 8: Answering a Phone Call 153
Chapter 9: Freefall 155
Chapter 10: The Final Statement of Belief 159

Section 2, Part II
Peter

Chapter 1: The Blame Game 165
Chapter 2: Tick Tick Tick 169
Chapter 3: Hide and Seek 171
Chapter 4: Discharge Meeting 173

Section 2, Part III
Lucky

Chapter 1: Start/Stop 179
Chapter 2: Anonymous 183
Chapter 3: All Apologies 191
Chapter 4: Nashville 195
Chapter 5: Heavenly Father 199
Chapter 6: Reflections Of 203
Chapter 7: Direct Communication 207
Chapter 8: A Perfect Storm Starting 211
Chapter 9: Hotel Happening 215
Chapter 10: Shooter 219
Chapter 11: The Road to the Road to 221
Chapter 12: The Theme from M*A*S*H* 227

Section 2, Part IV
Bobby-Joe

Chapter 1: Acceptance Speech 233
Chapter 2: No Comment, No Meaningt 237
Chapter 3: Backward 239

Section 3
The Shooter

Chapter 1: Lucky 243
Chapter 2: The Walk 247
Chapter 3: They Do Not Ring Out 249
Chapter 4: Standing Helplessly 253
Chapter 5: The Reluctant Hero 257

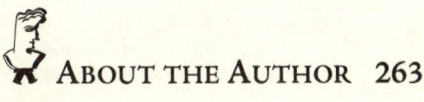

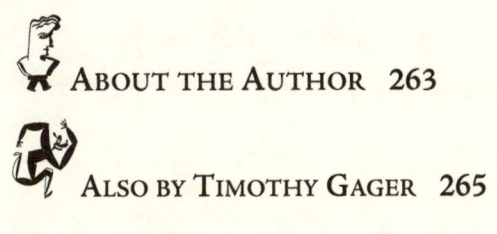

ABOUT THE AUTHOR 263

ALSO BY TIMOTHY GAGER 265

FOREWORD
Seamus McGraw

America's First Modern Mass Shooting Never Really Ended

The stench of burnt powder hung in the air as the elevator doors opened, knocking Ramiro Martinez back on his heels for an instant. Having muttered a desperate Hail Mary to himself, the off-duty Austin police officer rushed into the observatory of the Tower at the University of Texas, where a depraved killer, armed with a Remington 700, a shotgun, an M1 rifle and a grudge against the world, had rained bullets down on the "Forty Acres" for nearly 90 minutes.

Eleven were dead on the ground. Thirty-one were wounded. Inside the tower, three people had been killed, and two others wounded.

The truth is what began on the UT campus two generations ago has never ended. It's been repeated again and again, including in Killeen (23 dead, 1991), Fort Hood (13 dead, 2009), Sutherland Springs (26 dead, including an unborn child, 2017), Santa Fe (10 dead, 2018), El Paso (23 dead, 2019), Midland-Odessa (seven dead, four weeks later) and Uvalde, where 19 schoolchildren and two educators were killed on Tuesday by a teenage gunman.

In the years since the slaughter began, we've cobbled together a patchwork of comforting myths to explain the atrocities we've witnessed. In the case of the UT shooter, we cling to the theory that a tumor caused Whitman to murder his wife and 15 other innocent people. Though he did indeed have a brain tumor, it has never been conclusively proven that it was the tumor that led him to carefully plan and meticulously execute his mass murder.

We've blamed it on mental illness, ignoring the fact that 40 percent of mass shooters did not show signs or receive a diagnosis of mental illness, according to the National Alliance on Mental Illness. Make no mistake, there is a benefit to the attention that is focused on this nation's inadequate mental health system in the wake of these atrocities. But it's a collateral benefit, at best, and it risks stigmatizing the vast majority of people with mental illness—1 in 5 Americans—who are far more likely to be victims of crime than perpetrators.

We blame it on broken families, or absent fathers, ignoring the fact that in the case of the Austin Tower killer, his father was perhaps the single most influential person in his upbringing. Whitman's father was a looming presence in his life, rigid and authoritarian. He provided his family with all the comforts postwar America could offer but made sure that they understood that all its blessings flowed directly from him. Born in 1941, Whitman was raised in a typical nuclear family at the dawn of the nuclear age, though his parents' marriage did fall apart a few months before the shooting.

We blame bullying and childhood trauma. It is true that a third of all mass shooters have experienced severe childhood trauma, and that the figure is far higher (68%) among school shooters, according to The Violence Project's database of mass shootings in the United States from 1966 to 2019. There is no question that childhood trauma must be among the factors considered when assessing the various impulses and experiences that combine to turn a person into a mass shooter. But it's also true, as the communications researcher Casey Kelly has noted, that what many of these killers have claimed as victimization is sometimes little more than their own experience of run-of-the-mill disappointments and frustrations.

We blame violent video games for creating these killers, overlooking the fact that the killer at Sandy Hook Elementary School in Newtown, Connecticut in 2012—the only American school shooting deadlier than last week's in Uvalde—counted "Dance Dance Revolution" and the Mario Bros. as his favorite games.

And when all those other explanations fail, we turn to the theological, envisioning the killers as the personification of evil, and imagining that the good among us will ultimately prevail over them as part of an epic struggle that has been going on since before the world began. It's a word we've used time and again to describe these atrocities. When a gunman opened fire on congregants at a Fort Worth church in 1999, killing seven, then-Gov. George W. Bush laid the blame on a "wave of evil" sweeping the land. The hero of the 2017 Sutherland Springs massacre, who confronted the gunman outside a church where 26 people (including an unborn child) had been killed, later told me that he felt he was confronting the embodiment of "pure evil."

It is not surprising that, faced with mounting atrocities, we cast about for a silver bullet to explain away all the ones made of lead, a single, simple solution, or, failing that, a myth to make the slaughter more comprehensible. That's human nature.

Nor should it be surprising that so many of these myths can trace their roots to the atrocity at the University of Texas, and our efforts to comprehend the ongoing slaughter. Texas is a mythic place, and the myths that begin here have always become the myths of America.

But of all the myths and tropes that were born of fire that first day of August 1966, none has been more durable, or more deadly, than this: the notion that we can counter this unfathomable horror with heavily armed heroes who will rise spontaneously from our midst to save us.

It's the "good guy with a gun" myth. It was not fashioned out of whole cloth. Built upon our long and dark obsession with firearms, an indispensable part of the myth of Texas and, by extension, the myth of America, it was finally turned into a catchphrase by the National Rifle Association's Wayne LaPierre and marketed ruthlessly in the aftermath of the slaughter at Sandy Hook. And it had its first test at the University of Texas. The results were, to put it bluntly, inconclusive.

To be sure, there were those who rose to the challenge of the moment that day. And in the lore that's developed since, we've come to celebrate the memory of those students and everyday citizens who ran home to fetch their hunting rifles and unleashed a barrage against the tower, while McCoy, Martinez and Crum edged toward the killer perched on the parapet with his long-range Remington.

It is indeed possible that the fire from the ground may have forced the murderer to take cover behind the balustrade and impeded his ability to aim and fire, saving some lives. But it is just as likely that the fire from the ground impeded the ability of those heroic first responders to confront and kill Whitman. As Martinez told me just a couple of years ago, "Bullets kept coming at us, they crack—you could hear the crack as they go over your head and then they'd hit the tower. Dust would come down, rain down in little particles of stone."

In the decades since the slaughter in Austin, decades that have seen our streets flooded with weapons capable of firing far more deadly rounds at a far faster rate than the now almost quaint rifle used by the ex-Marine in the tower, the trope has been tested time and time and time again, and it has almost always come up wanting.

Indeed, out of 277 gun massacres examined by the FBI between 2000 and 2018 in three studies, so-called good guys with guns interrupted mass shootings 3.9% of the time. Unarmed civilians interrupted them almost three times more often (11.9%). And 27% of the time, it was a bad guy with a gun—the killer himself—who ended the rampage by killing himself.

Yet we cling to the myth of the good guy with the gun; we've made it almost an article of faith. Indeed, it is now so deeply rooted in us that even the killers themselves use it to justify their slaughters, motivated as they almost always are by some grievance, some sense of victimhood, some narcissistic, delusional vision of themselves as heroes or avengers. That was driven home to me not so terribly long ago when, while interviewing a killer, now serving life in prison for a 1992 mass shooting at Bard College at Simon's Rock in Massachusetts* that claimed three lives and would have claimed more had the semiautomatic rifle he bought on his 18th birthday not jammed, I asked him whether a good guy with a gun would have stopped him. "I thought I was the good guy with the gun," he replied.

Set aside for a moment, if you can, the unspeakable grief and shame that we as a nation should feel every time we look at photographs of the innocent victims of these massacres. Forget for a moment the anguish of their loved ones. Consider this instead: the trauma etched in the faces of the first responders who we thrust, poorly prepared, into the bloody epicenter of these atrocities.

You can hear the impact in the voice of a veteran police officer, a member of one of the teams who first entered the classrooms at Sandy Hook, who was so overwhelmed by what he saw that he simply erased the memory, and when investigators asked him, he insisted that he never set foot inside, one of those investigators later told me. You can feel the awful weight of it in the voice of a young police officer, summoned to Sante Fe High School, in the Houston area, during a mass shooting there, holding the line outside the school while his own mother was dying inside. In his grief, his family's lawyer told me, the officer cried out: "I'm supposed to protect and serve people, I couldn't even protect my own mother!"

Indeed, in our devotion to the idea that "the only thing that can stop a bad guy with a gun is a good guy with a gun," we are asking our police and first responders, our EMTs and our firefighters, to face horrors on their home turf as great as any they'd find on the bloodiest foreign battlefield. We haven't asked American soldiers to do that in their own country, at least since the Civil War, yet we demand it of these first responders. As the psychology researcher Deborah C. Beidel from the University of Central Florida, who has studied the impact these slaughters have on first responders, put it, "There are just some events that are so horrific that no human being should be able to just process that and put it away." And when, as we saw in Uvalde, our officers, our defenders, fail for whatever reason to rise to the moment, we vilify them, and call them cowards. That, too, is part of the myth of the good guy with the gun, the notion that the world is binary, neatly divided into heroes and cowards. It isn't.

But if you know what a bullet from an AR-15 can do to an adult body, then you can understand, if not forgive, that commander for imagining that after 100 rounds fired at close range, there would be no child left in the room to save, even if they stormed it. No number of heroes, no number of good guys with guns can adequately respond to a field of fire like that. The best you can do is react. And you can never react in time.

Almost certainly, there will be a demand for accountability for that delay in doing so. But if we're going to indict those officers, even if only in the court of public opinion, then we also have an obligation to indict ourselves. Even now, before the bodies of those 19 children and two teachers are buried, there are the perfectly predictable calls to double down on the myth of the good guy with a gun. Just as there were after Santa Fe and El Paso and Midland-Odessa and countless others, there are renewed calls to simply flood the zone with more guns, in the perfect and simplistic faith that untested and inexperienced civilians, teachers, custodians will somehow miraculously arise against depraved killers armed with weapons of war.

That's not a plan. That's not a policy. That's theology. There are far more AR-15s and far more rounds of ammunition that can vaporize flesh, shatter bone and explode internal organs than there are heroes. And if that is the only response to the ever-mounting slaughter of this nation's children and its grandparents, and its congregations at worship, and its crowds at movie theaters and country music concerts, then we don't have a prayer.

Seamus McGraw
August, 2024

Full text, The Texas Tribune, June 1, 2022
Truncated version used by permission

McGraw is an avid deer hunter who, from mid-October to late January, rarely ventures out from his home in the mountains of Pennsylvania without a rifle in his hand. These days, he exclusively carries a .50-caliber flintlock. He is also the author of *From a Taller Tower: The Rise of the American Mass Shooter*, published last year by the University of Texas Press.

America's First Modern Mass Shooting Never Really Ended originally appeared in *The Texas Tribune* and is used here by permission.

The Texas Tribune is a member-supported, nonpartisan newsroom informing and engaging Texans on state politics and policy. Learn more at texastribune.org.

Shadows Of The Seen

PROLOGUE

They Do Not Ring Out

Shots do not ring out, they pop. Whoever says ring out never has been in an outdoor area with gunfire raging, where you are cursing God for the unfortunate location you are in. If you describe gunfire ringing out, you are a bad poet, songwriter, or newscaster. Anyone who knows anything about the sound of gunfire will describe it as a pop, like small fireworks, during the exact moment your mind tries to determine what exactly it hears.

Most of the time the mind is too busy with denial, convinced it is fireworks... some kids involved in a prank. That denial is quickly overruled, for why would there be screaming if it's just a string of firecrackers the size of a pack of cigarettes. Pop-pop-pop. Once you have adjusted for denial you quickly scan the location looking for a shooter. You tell yourself a shooter will be wearing military garb, perhaps black in color, definitely wearing a heavy, bulletproof vest. The shooter would be dressed the same way a member of a SWAT team would when defending people from a cold-blooded killer with a semi-automatic.

Then you see him, because your mind has tricked you again—he is just wearing a light t-shirt and jeans, with a well-worn, fatigue-patterned hat. You think if you must describe him later, it is a false memory of the Los Angeles Dodgers, Kansas City Royals. or New York Mets. You are the only person within 500 yards, as there is not a parting of a Red Sea of people falling like bowling pins between you and him. Not yet, and even so, they might not see him. The other people are a distance away, but still not safe. He now opens fire. Pop-pop-pop.

It is just your dumb luck that you're in this position, the one of you and him. Then you think, what happens if he turns around and shoots you? Will it be quick? Will it hurt? Maybe it will just blow your head off. But also, what happens if he does and you just don't give a fuck. I mean, life's not been all that good, so no harm, but foul? Definitively foul.

Instead of your life flashing before your eyes, the thoughts are more concrete. You think you will not be missed. You've told yourself that so many times, right after you have told yourself that it might be useful being hospitalized to adjust your mental health, but the depression and thoughts of negative self-worth will just pop up once more. You never act on it; it never changes and nothing seems to help. People suggest you talk about it. What has always stopped you is those thoughts are so hard to explain to others. Just observe others having trouble after, say, a suicide. You remember a friend who did it forty-or so years ago, and his now eighty-year-old parents are still trying to explain it. They are trying to find the answer, still trying to crack the case.

You and a lone shooter. People are far away, but your main discomfort isn't him, it is the wind and cold drizzle.

He is still not turning around, not seeing you, as he walks toward Broadway shooting, bullets ricocheting off buildings, cars, and striking a few people at a distance, not knowing what hit them, the chaos beginning, the screaming now a sustained din. You know you could escape, but you also know that there is nothing left for you to lose, just your life, which as you check in again, is still the same nothing it was a minute ago. And the shooter is still fifty yards away, walking... walking... walking. And suddenly, you find yourself running; the distance between you and the shooter seems to be halved in every step you take, like a runaway roller coaster descending from the upmost peak of the ride, never slowing down. Why are you doing this? You are a stride away, and the shooter still has not turned to face you... and he will not pivot, or fire off some rounds and kill you. It is not going to happen right now, because he can't. You are upon him. You lower your head and bury your right shoulder as hard as you can into the center of his t-shirt between his scapula, the semi-automatic weapon firing randomly before nose diving, muzzle straight down into the cement, the force from all this ejecting the gun away from him.

Section 1, Part I

Candace

1

The Nicene Creed

The Nicene Creed is one of the most famous and influential creeds in the history of the church, because it settled the question of how Christians can worship one God and also claim that this God is three persons.

A majority of people believe in one thing, the Almighty conclusions of the seen and unseen. They believe in one church and will go down fighting for that vision. The parents of Representative Candace Malone were True Believers, though Candace was pretty much an atheist but kept mostly silent about it. As a Republican she believed the absolutes of voting demographics trump every thought and credence she might have. She knew her career meant either winning or going home. She believed in talking about church, state, Pro-Life, and the United States of America. She believed anything that would get her into office was worth the disingenuousness.

She inherited those fundamentalist values, as well as the color of hair, brown, and eyes, a brilliant green, from her parents, Matthew Taylor, a Judge in Chattanooga County, and Mary, "just a housewife," as she later would refer to herself in interviews. Candace was taught about the darkness and the light and having no crossover, no gray area. Matthew and Mary even chose her name because it meant "clarity and whiteness." It made Candace feel off center, one-sided, and at times hidden.

What was it that the Taylors wanted to hide? Were there things in the world that weren't up to par? Were there things in their own lives which needed to be kept under a blanket? Of course, there were. There were things embarrassing or which the people of God would disapprove of behind their black, glossy front doors in their beautiful homes.

It started when Candace was in middle school, a thin fifteen year old, with long, straight brown hair that seemed to border her statuesque body. There was a boy, a wonderful boy, she had said in her diary, who paid attention to her, but no one paid much attention to him.

"We can do this. I'd like you to be my boyfriend," she said to him, "but my parents can never find out about it."

Peter Botchovich had no real relationship with his own parents except the one where he physically and mentally defended himself from their wrath, so his response, "That's fine," was pretty easy. Peter didn't understand the concept of parents at all.

Being a secret boyfriend made him much more exciting to her. Mostly he was wonderful to her because he *was* a boyfriend, an actual bona fide boyfriend. There was nothing better than when endorphins for love kicked in, a clandestine first love that kept her blind, made him better than he was.

She and Peter, a shy athlete, not in with any crowd, planned meetings where no one would catch them. They had top-secret kisses and touched each other in the shadows of the hallway's corners, behind pillars, and in the locked, single-room bathroom located near the principal's office. The plan was always to meet 28 minutes after the period started, and then entering the private bathroom one at a time.

Candace couldn't wait. She loved having Peter's arms wrapped around her, and even grew to love the background, with the smell of cheap, germ-eliminating industrial cleaner the janitor used. After they left, one at a time, there was the smell of sweet sweat and sex, Candace adjusting her dress, sweeping her damp, slick hair off her face.

After some instances she realized the obligation. She had to be there to quell the anticipation and demand for seeing him. There was also the nervousness of her not being able to sneak out to meet him at any given time. She did not wish to be the cause of Peter being mad or acting unpredictably for the next couple of days. She had to be wherever he said, at the time he stated, otherwise there would be some hell, or guilt, or explanation about where she was instead. When it couldn't happen, Candace didn't know if it would end in him being angry, or jealous, or both. Candace felt this was what love and being cared for was all about, but Candace didn't know. All she wanted was for him to forgive her and touch her face softly, sweep her soft hair back away from her eyes.

Another place they would see each other was at church, much less exciting, much more damning. Candace and Peter always had attended the same church, which was where they first caught each other's eyes. Peter noticed her hair, her thick, straight hair of brown. Both their parents had wondered about the sudden interest in dressing well, or in Peter's parents' case, even him not being forced to go, as he had stated that once he had reached a certain age, church was one of the things he would cut out of his life. It was a way to rebel, to have control over something regarding his parents. Mostly he just felt lost around them, but certainly and unpredictably, Peter continued to attend and act less sullen.

On a Sunday, when his parents headed to the car, he saw Candace headed downstairs to the church basement alone. This was his chance to get to talk to her. Peter said he wanted to get a donut and would be right back. Candace, in a yellow dress was *near* the donut table, but Peter couldn't hold back in approaching. He did not want to chicken out and take the easy way out—which was grabbing a donut and not saying anything. He stopped directly in front of her, face-to-face, no more than three feet away, handed her a donut, and paused, then froze, meeting her gaze and her own pause and fear head-on.

"Hey, I know you from school," he said.

"Uh, huh," she nodded, and smiled, holding back a giggle which turned into a laugh when he suddenly scurried away.

Back in the car his parents asked, "Where's the fucking donut you wasted our time to get?"

"Ate it," he said.

On the Monday after, Candace tapped his shoulder as he was opening his locker. "Hey, I know you from church," she said.

"Yes, you do," was his response. "See you there?"

"Before that?" she asked, surprised at her own bravery.

"After school?"

"OK."

They also continued to see each other in church. The sermons were considered appropriate, one on "Remaining Pure for God", was followed up by the next week's "How Un-pure Thoughts are Indeed Sins". The pastor noted that, "You can't hold the hand of God if you are using yours for something else. It is how one gets morally off-center."

Candace silently objected to both the words *pure* one week, and *indeed* the next. *Nothing is pure,* she thought, and *indeed is such a stupid word.* She pictured a pair of old couples saying stupid things, usually said by the husbands, with the wives just responding with the non-conflictual, "Indeed." She received a harsh look from her parents when she smirked at the pastor's *immoral use of hands* comment. Peter sat mostly staring at her, not processing a single word from the sermon, and getting turned on by thinking of using his hands on young Candace Taylor.

But something the church and their parents didn't know was that indeed more and more things were getting off-centered. It was more than Candace and Peter's unmonitored use of more than their hands on each other, a by-product of the romance, believed by Peter to be on the high end of the Romeo and Juliet scale, except the real opposition to their relationship was only from Peter himself.

What Peter believed was the amazing Candace certainly was worthy of love, but Peter was the one not worthy of her. Deep inside of Peter, he disapproved of himself, but knew he loved Candace with all that he had. It was a huge conflict, given Peter's thinking that no one could possibly love him. Yet, lines had already been crossed which the church and the Taylors had drawn, and things had advanced from just making out in their secret hiding place at school to having sex in there, pushing each other's bodies against the sanitized tile.

So, it wasn't like Romeo and Juliet. It was past that. Candace became sick in the morning. She knew exactly what that meant, but she had no idea what to do or how to handle it. When she told Peter, he didn't have anything much to say about what to do or even what it would mean in their lives. The pregnancy had crossed a line, and Candace wouldn't report back to the church, but she felt a guilty need to report to her parents. She had made the decision, against Peter's strong objection, because her parents would find out soon enough, either by catching her being sick, which could easily be lied about only once or twice, or her beginning to show.

Sitting on the living room sofa across from her parents, Candace felt she had no defense from the shame and humiliation she was feeling. Although Peter was angry this was happening, she didn't feel scared or intimidated by him. He had no solution for this either and they both knew it. Her green eyes glazed over when she confessed her mistake.

The gears in the heads of Matthew and Mary turned quickly and immediately. Neither of them spoke right away, which surprised Candace, but somehow their silence seemed even worse. Even if they were mad, they seemed to be strategizing first, maybe showing emotion later. Candace realized that her pregnancy was something that they, as Christians, could not be associated with. The Taylors needed to hide this, to get rid of it.

Matthew and Mary needed a plan that wouldn't ruin everything in their and their daughter's present and future lives, so they, without talking to Candace, came up with one without her. The Taylors decided that as long as there was a negative moral association and shame around a pregnant 15 year old, there might as well be a very immoral solution, which would solve the problem. It was a solution they could all keep secret. And after it all happened, they could pray to be forgiven. That was part of the plan, to pray, and pray, and pray, until they felt forgiven enough, if that was to be at all possible.

They also knew that there could be no record of this. If there were a paper trail, and this would be known, then the best-case scenario of that would be full ostracizing of them, with a pinch or worse of shame. The worst case? Reputations and careers, current and future, would be ruined, and the family would need to remove

Candace from school, moving to a location far from home for a fresh start.

So, they rented a car where no one could discover them, made an appointment at Planned Parenthood, and took her to get an abortion. The Taylors used all the power and privilege they held in their city of Chattanooga, Tennessee, to have it scheduled in the middle of the night, where there would be no sign-carrying fundamentalists holding up pictures of bloody fetuses, or possibly recognizing them. No one would have this opportunity, which would give Candace any future she wished because, after all, America is the land of opportunity. She later stated this in her Governor's acceptance speech, twenty-five years from this point about America, but certainly not about Pro-Choice, as she never really had one. She also spouted a truth, one which ignored the real truth of her life, so that she could give a true red, white, and blue message. "Even at fifteen, I had a life vision, one in which I would become the first female President of the United States."

Her dream still could be lived, but this was far away from the night at the clinic where there were no cheers, when her long, soft brown hair became matted from her tears.

2

The Politics of Men

After her abortion, with honors graduation from high school, Candace would receive a full scholarship to Vanderbilt University. Her essay captured her dream and desire to be the first woman president, and it also struck a chord with the enrollment specialist who was drawn to Candace's sincere objective to not allow politics to affect her personal life. She studied Political Science as a steppingstone toward her goal. She no longer wore her hair long, but rather in a mature, conservative length, with a part on the side.

While at Vanderbilt, she met a "safe" man, with good strong features, and moussed black hair, who looked good in a well-tailored suit. Bobby-Joe Malone was brought up by Evangelist parents (all the God, but not so much the Rapture), was still a virgin, and was the President of the Young Republicans Club. Candace, brought up Republican, still didn't know where she stood exactly, but the second Bobby-Joe handed her a flyer which invited her to a Young Republicans Club meeting, her lean shifted quickly to that direction. *Men, she thought, men... ugh, the gateway to society's decision making*, whether they made good decisions or bad. Justifiably, she knew she needed a man at some point to be her unofficial running mate, but she knew to take it one step at a time. First, she would have to ask Bobby-Joe out.

Candace felt the best thing about Bobby-Joe was that he was not at all like Peter. Her parents would love him, which was important, because she never completely recovered their trust since, as they put it, *that unfortunate incident*. They would be pleased with his sexual status, even though Candace was not. There was something about sneaking around, which she'd had with Peter, that would flip the excitement switch in Candace, creating a strong desire to change Bobby-Joe, to corrupt him, to make him want her. Bobby-Joe stayed true to his beliefs, and she never was able to get what she wanted with him.

It was the reason, when she felt weak, she still stayed in touch with Peter. It was always with late night phone calls, saying things to him she should never say and listening to him getting off to them. Immediately she would hang up to take care of her own needs, but then it was the shame which overwhelmed her, swearing to herself she would never do it again, bringing her back to Bobby-Joe.

Then it would all wear off, and Candace would call Peter after midnight. When he would try to call her, she would always let it go to the answering-machine, with the messages being left, as her roommate noted, concerning. The concerning messages were overwhelm-ing and controlling, the way men with small levels of self-confidence would become abusive. It gave her a reason to call him back, to chastise him, and then win him back over in the way she always did.

Bobby-Joe again was the opposite of Peter. He had

the confidence but did not need the pressure of a relationship at this time, even though he and Candace would be seen nearly every day with one another, meeting for lunch and attending University functions and parties. Candace's hand would often slip into Bobby-Joe's, which seemed very unimposing and a natural occurrence.

Bobby-Joe would use his degree in Architecture from Vandy to go to Harvard, and later use his skills to make a valuable contribution to the Nashville skyline as an up-and-coming star, a yellow boy amongst the average. Bobby-Joe was driven. Peter, on the other hand, was stuck on the ground, looking up at the ladder of success.

It was easy logically for Candace to move on, but it was not an easy decision. It was time to completely remove herself from Peter, which by physical distance shouldn't have been that hard to do, but it was the emotional part. She thought long and hard about her future. It was only then, when she became more distant, no longer calling him, it become totally clear how controlling and toxic Peter actually was. His messages seemed crazy, an unrealistic shattering. She prayed that maybe time would fade Peter's obsession with her. Maybe he would meet someone else. All she knew was that she didn't want to date anyone else. It was nice having Bobby-Joe as a friend, a confidant, and someone who would make a good partner for her career, far away in Massachusetts. This made it much easier being distant from him than it ever was from Peter.

While in graduate school, Candace and Bobby-Joe kept in touch via email but did not see each other during that time. She knew to Bobby-Joe she had to be a lifetime relationship, a commitment because of who he was. Candace respected that. His beliefs rang out to her as very true, noble, and honorable. After all, wasn't being a virgin a part of all this, the final outcome being partnership? She imagined his penis was like the bottle in the game. Spin the bottle; wherever it would land was exactly who he would end up with. It could have landed on her, but it just spun indefinitely. Candace knew there wouldn't be a re-spin if it had stopped, because as things were, it was more about him and less about her. When he returned to Tennessee, there seemed to be even less contact, and then none.

It wasn't until years later, when she ran for Governor of Tennessee, they were to be reacquainted. It happened at one of her fundraising cocktail parties, and though Bobby-Joe would never admit it to her, in the same way Candace would never admit her abortion he, after all these years, pined for her. Still a virgin, Bobby-Joe's thoughts were as sinful and graphic as Candace's old calls to Peter; having thoughts of her pushing him down, and being on top of him, forcefully riding God away from him. At the fundraiser, as an up-and-coming star for the city, he was let in without an invitation. When he tapped her on the shoulder, she at first flinched, a hard defensive reflex, as if something bad was about to go down. Her first thought was that it was Peter, who had threatened and manipulated her after her detachment. He was always in her thoughts. The touch sent a shiver right down her spine. But here was Bobby-Joe standing in front of her once more, and all she felt was a desire to collapse into his arms. Candace knew right then and there that Bobby-Joe meant more to her than she had ever thought. He was the right choice. She knew it, and it didn't matter he had not been directly in her life in a long time. She knew he was the one who had more of the characteristics of a life-partner to propel her into office—and he was handsome, moral, and a known entity in the state of Tennessee. Initially, it took Candace's team additional time to screen Bobby-

Joe, to confirm he still had strong beliefs and no skeletons in his closet which might harm her. Her pollsters and research groups revealed if she was neutral on any issue, someone exactly like Bobby-Joe would stimulate her voter base.

Bobby-Joe was also a tried-and-true Republican who could fill the void painted by the press of her being alone, single, no partner in sight. He also had the ability to fill other voids, being strongly spoken on some key Republican issues. On the topic of guns, Candace had trouble with Bobby-Joe's views, strongly based on the incorrect Pro-Second Amendment talking point. Her own opinion, somewhat Anti-violent, had always been deflected as non-committal to the voters, and many undecided registered Republicans started to look at other candidates. Her lack of religious rhetoric was eased by having Bobby-Joe, whom everyone loved as a mouthpiece. Candace didn't necessarily like it. *He's not saying exactly where I stand*, she thought. He, very often, was viewed to be just as important as she, the actual candidate. After all, in the openly misogynistic world in which she traveled that might be a plus. On the campaign trail, it often made her want to scream. Bobby-Joe's having different beliefs from hers was by-and-by OK with her, only if it helped her career. She could privately disagree, publicly love, and keep her eye on the prize, playing it for all it was worth. The more and more she was seen next to Bobby-Joe, the more her poll numbers rose.

She also played the Anti-intelligence card which voters seem to respond to, even though she and Bobby-Joe were both very intelligent. It was better to act as if she weren't. Candace also knew what could create a challenge in her run. Her former ties with Peter Botchovich might be a problem. As her campaign became more public, what if he decided to appear as well? What if he had an axe to grind and wanted to use her abortion as some sort of blackmail scheme. She knew he had potential to be vindictive, but she just wasn't sure how far he would go. She called her parent's family lawyer and spoke to them and her parents all at once. If those loose ends with Peter were to be tied up, what was necessary was additional money to Peter, and a Non-Disclosure Agreement, in which nothing could be said about Candace, the abortion, or their past relationship.

Peter understood completely, and nothing had to be explained, as it was all pretty obvious. He had been through this before. The agreement came to a good amount of money, and an additional no-contact order. He could never be found out about or brought in out of the woodwork, or even be "accidently" seen within the same location as Candace Taylor. The order was the polar opposite of what she had with Bobby-Joe, who was rapidly becoming a large aspect of the campaign, glued to her with the strongest adhesion possible.

Preparedness-wise, Candace ran a solid campaign. She researched exactly what people wanted to see or hear, and she fed it to them. She funded countless focus groups, which mostly came back with the obvious Republican agenda for vote getting—guns, religion, rights, freedoms. The groups also informed her that as a woman in the south, she needed to look good, and strong, but not come off as "too powerful." This was a big political sway point. Hell, even women as attractive as Candace would be found, according to focus groups, less attractive if they came on too strong in the non-political world. She wanted to avoid the *GOP bitch persona*, and in the more aggressive sector of both parties, *a GOP cunt*. Another one of her focus groups informed her of that.

Every day she would do a check-in with Bobby-Joe to push back the bulldog in her. Each check-in involved pausing and breathing exercises, as well as Bobby-Joe firing loaded, rapid-fire questions in her direction that she could answer firmly, confidently, and also pausing, to not appear too excited, even with the issues she was the most excited about. The polls and focus groups indicated that being a hard working, Type-A personality in her geographical area would be viewed as positive traits, but not that important of a variable for a woman looking for votes. Being passive and somewhat traditional in the way gender roles always have been was the winning combination. She hated that.

"Sometimes you just have to eat a little political shit," Bobby-Joe would tell her during foreplay and immediately before she did a move he liked, slipping her panties to the side and climbing on top of him.

Sometimes I actually have to eat your shit, she thought, his conversation ruining the possibility of her orgasming.

"Can't I just fix things? Make them better?" she asked, sweeping her hair away from the front of her face.

"No. Sometimes you just have to eat a lot of other shit, babe," he said as she suddenly rolled off him before either of them had even really started.

3

Votes

Those following the race couldn't help but feel that Bobby-Joe was a big piece of the campaign to success. Candace realized having a "First Man," could only do so much, but his being hands-on was a bonus in her numbers. She knew Bobby-Joe had to be active, a support partner, but more importantly be seen as a co-candidate, to the misogynistic demographic she was dealing with. It's what the focus groups, and now the polls, told her. She hated all the people in the focus groups for the kind of stupid that gnawed at her.

She reasoned that she was more of a director, moving Bobby-Joe's location as the window dressing whenever there was the time and place for that. Also, if she wanted him to stand out, and be the strutting peacock, he would. He was good at it, and as a couple they brought the appearance of being two young, attractive, and well put together people. Questions about the future infrastructure of the state would be deferred to Bobby-Joe. This was something more acceptable to Candace. After all, he was a star in the architectural world, and the entire Tennessee skyline was not the limit for someone like him. Bobby-Joe could always go further with ease, and people wanted to believe that their own communities could be updated and have the same potential in the exact same positive progression the cities Bobby-Joe had influenced. Nashville had been a success in the same way people update their I-phones, with cell-phone companies offering everything for free, but in actuality it wasn't. Nothing is free, and things that looked too good to be true, usually were. Also, if you went against your own beliefs, the new opposite ones may come back and bite you.

Another thing which was referred to Bobby-Joe was the gun issue. On that, she didn't quite know what to do yet. Tennessee was currently a red state with the trend heading to that at a greater and greater numbers, which put the gun issue in line to Second Amendment rhetoric. What Candace actually believed was that mass shootings were senseless and couldn't be stopped the way society was set up. Even if people had guns, no one in their right minds should be owning assault weapons. She would love to speak up about the 70% less likely occurrences of mass shootings fatalities during the federal assault weapons ban which had been lifted. These high-powered weapons never seemed to stop other shootings, which was an argument, or used to protect oneself, which was another. They all seemed to go to the bad guys, the ones of pure evil, who couldn't be stopped with any amount of good guys with guns, who would be said to conveniently pop up on site whenever something bad was about to go down.

"You can't talk about renewing the ban," Bobby-Joe warned her. "What you can talk about is, what if the entire country was carrying?"

"What if...?" she asked with alarm. "Do you actually believe in arming everyone?"

"Anything more moderate will lose you votes, and the race is neck-and-neck. I could tweet about arming everyone. That will help."

"Jesus Christ. It's not what I believe," she countered. "That's madness. Don't make me regret that I gave you the keys to my Twitter account."

"Well, you can sit at home with your beliefs, or you can govern the great state of Tennessee," Bobby-Joe said, and she knew he had her.

"Gak," was her best response, knowing it was a lose-lose to stick with her beliefs and to fight with him on them. "You know what else would help in the polls?" she asked, her voice trailing off as she ran her hand down the padded shoulder of his suit down to his elbow.

"Oh, are you talking about those polls, or my poll?" he laughed.

"You're an idiot," she countered, then suddenly more serious, said. "I know we agreed to wait, but this could be huge for the campaign. Here's what I thought." She continued to massage the bend of his elbow with a firm hand, and then he understood exactly what she was getting at.

"Ut, oh."

"Here's what I thought," she began.

"We don't have time right now. I mean, the election."

Oh, my God, he can be such a prick, she thought. "Are you going to let me finish?" she said instead, and waited for Bobby-Joe to nod, because usually when he nodded, he was all-in for listening and considering. "We do it at the Justice of the Peace, and then have a surprise announcement... hell, we could walk down the street of the courthouse in a tuxedo and gown. People love surprises. What an opportunity to be seen!"

"But, what do you want? You always talked about having a real wedding, the kind you'd imagined as a girl. Many bridesmaids, a horse-pulled carriage, rose petals, a gown with a long train...."

"I want to win this thing is what I want. After I win this thing, we will have a huge reception with family, friends, reporters... the most influential people in the state. We can do it at the State House, maybe Live-Tweet it. It's a win-win."

"Are you sure?"

"No holding back," she insisted.

There was a moment of brief silence, then she pushed her palm against the front of his shoulder, pivoting him to face her. "Bobby-Joe Malone. Will you take Ms. Candace Taylor's hand and marry her, for God's sake?"

Bobby-Joe leaned in and gave her a long kiss, which she let herself enjoy for a few seconds before she pulled away. "Wait, no one said 'you may kiss the bride'."

"May I?"

"I'll wait until you say 'I do'," she teased.

"Of course, I do," he said, and then it was her turn to lean in, and take charge of the next kiss.

4

Yes, Governor

Governor Candace Taylor-Malone coasted to victory. There were certain things which helped her win easily. Not only did she live-tweet and livestream her dressed-up walk down Court Street, but she responded to each and every comment after the videos were saved on the various social media platforms. The best advice ever for the internet, "don't read the comments," was ignored by Candace, who fired back at her haters, even the most superficial of them, the ones that commented on her appearance. These ranged from disgusting requests on what some man might do to her in bed to horrible blurbs saying that she was hideous looking, mostly from Democrats. Candace knew the logic that things can't be two completely different points-of-view at the same time, but still, the comments stung. To those she would respond, "I'm sure your spouse, or significant other, if you have one, is beautiful, both inside and out." To the perverted come-ons, Candace decided to handle those the same way Suzy Kolber took on a drunk Joe Namath who sloppily asked to kiss her, live, and on-the-air of a

Monday Night Football Game with just a simple, "Thanks," and saying the name of person, "that's such a compliment." It was tactics like these that made her relatable, exactly like her focus groups said.

Candace loved being governor, but she was still a little uncomfortable living in the Pro-Life, Pro-Gun, Pro-God world. She was gaining confidence in talking about all of those in the most advantageous way for her, but all-in-all she most reveled helping people and being in the public eye. She and Bobby-Joe were becoming more and more the people's choice. They were on the fast track for much bigger goals, and they both knew it. This didn't go unnoticed to the various influential lobbyists who began to approach her and take her and Bobby-Joe out for dinners, filling their ears with their own various needs. The largest, most powerful group was made up of gun lobbyists and members of the National Rifle Association.

"I know what they want already." she told Bobby-Joe afterward, "Why can't they just shut up about their agendas and let us have an enjoyable meal?"

"You know, babe, that's why we're getting the meal and... ,"

"Yes, that sometimes you have to eat a little shit."

"Actually, what I was going to say is that it's good for your career and good for us if you potentially align on their side of this one. It'll get you into a more powerful office, and financially give us a huge edge, either in campaign donations or just gift donations in general."

"I thought of that, and I'm OK with the campaign part of it, but the gifts? I don't believe in high-powered assault rifles, and I don't want to take bribes to...."

"Gifts," he corrected.

"I don't want to take gifts, then, to make my public align with me, even though I'm not exactly aligned with them."

"Either way, the amount of these gifts can approach close to a million dollars. That type of money would do a great service for getting you into The House of Representatives."

"To which I would have to make statements for and vote on things in a certain way I don't 100% agree with for the rest of my political life?"

"Again... or not have a life in politics."

She knew he was right. "Fuck," she said.

"Just win," Bobby-Joe replied.

5

Take the Money and Run

Candace took the money from the NRA and any other gun lobbyists, and she hated it. At least, when just a candidate, she didn't feel directly involved in every mass shooting as she did now. She also took from the Pro-Choice lobbyists, but even though she had had a secret abortion, she felt more comfortable accepting money from them. With abortion she felt some were justified, but others, it depended on where the line was drawn between the couple's all-around ability to have the child or not.

Most of all, Candace just didn't want to think about any of it. Shootings dominating the news, but Pro-Choice vs. Pro-Rights was just another messy debate, the same way religion and God were spoken about on the campaign trails. The most important thing she and Bobby-Joe knew was that the key votes were all about how her district felt about all these debates. The right to guns and the right to abort were the biggest two issues that determined which way Mr. and Mrs. Tennessee would go, even if Candace could never wrap her head around the idea that humans killed by guns were somehow less important than embryos aborted. Weren't they either both killed or both not killed?

Around this time there was a mall shooting in Minnesota, which left fifteen people dead and fourteen others wounded. The security guard, and two shoppers who tried to stop the shooter by charging were gunned down, re-opening the case for arming mall security guards, and other "good-guy" citizens. Candace knew that no matter how good they were with weapons, these shoppers could not defend society against a semi-automatic weaponed shooter, and tno mall would arm employees with enough fire power.

As a constantly active candidate, Candace dreaded having to make a statement on this and every fucking tragedy. She rehearsed in front of Bobby-Joe, to ward off any nervousness or the physical shaking which happened when she was anxious. By the time it was time to speak, she didn't shake. She had a backup plan in her head which was saying she was shaking out of anger, but that plan never needed to be invoked. Candace stuck with the rhetoric that it was catastrophic, senseless, and that it wasn't the guns doing the shooting, but rather, the shooter's mental state which was the most important aspect of all of this.

"Well, shouldn't there be stronger background checks? Do you support that?" a reporter from the *Chattanooga Times Free Press* asked.

"I support anything which would have averted this tragedy, including keeping such people off the street, the ones that kill. They need to be in places where they can't harm our children, our teachers, and all of the good people that live here in Tennessee."

She felt her voice crack when she answered. She thought it was showing weakness, but she was just over-thinking that everyone else had heard her, but actually no one had. To be safe she thanked the press, excused herself to head back to her office and locked the door. There it was safe to have a good long cry.

6

Enemies

Candace's Democratic opponents were strong on the Anti-gun, Pro-Choice agenda. Secretly, Candace, if she weren't running against them, could see being on board with their platform. The first opponent of note, Clint Billson, had the traditional southern style, slow and deliberate, with a prominent drawl, and excessively confident. He recently had a lot of his own secrets revealed when the key Democratic debates were just beginning. Out of the woodwork, a woman appeared stating that she had had an affair with Clint Billson, and the baby that was his responsibility was taking the fine citizens of Tennessee's tax money through welfare and food stamps. There was even a photo of Billson and the woman standing together at a NASCAR event. This was enough to knock an adamantly denying Clint down a notch in the polls until the woman ended up cracking under the pressure of the media. During the inter-rogation on this very buzzy story, the woman admitted that she had never met Clint Billson, except for the photo, and she was put up to this by Billson's opponent Ken Sannison.

It was true that Sannison had planted the woman to stir up some dirt, because he had thought the real threat for being elected was Clint Billson, not Candace Malone, on deck in the Republican wings for a future face off. When the woman came clean, it was Ken Sannison who took the hit, as the media screamed headlines, and the internet created click-bait about the wrinkly, overweight Sannison, complete with uncompli-mentary photos of him shoving an entire Popeye's fried chicken breast into his mouth. With Sannison down for the count, Candace got what she thought was a lucky break.

A second woman came out, touting the bravery of the first, who wasn't brave at all, as a different person with a child conceived with Clint Billson. Not to be hoodwinked again, the media called for a DNA test, comparing it to Billson's DNA drawn off a podium.

It came back a match.

Now Candace was going to walk into the House of Representatives speaking only about her own morals to start and also about Pro-gun, Pro-Life for the cherry on top. What she didn't take into account was that while Ken Sannison was sloppy—which according to the polls made him doubly unlikeable after the fake paternity set-up, Clint Billson was generally a smooth talker and influencer.

The strategy Clint Billson took was to admit everything child-related; not apologize, and appear as genuine about this as possible. "After all, this is the kind of stuff which happens in life," he said, adding, "but we do not shirk away from our responsibilities. We, as Americans, are accountable, and we take care of our messes." During this, he was shirking big-time because he was being very clever to stay on course of being an electable human being.

Mr. Responsibility, Clint Billson, was then photographed, along with his wife, bringing children's gifts and money to the woman who had revealed the real act of infidelity. There was an issue that the gifts brought for his blood-child were about five to ten years away from being age-inappropriate, the gifts suiting a much younger child.

"You can return these, honey," Bill's wife, Millicent, said with a smile so tight that one could only remove the terseness of it with Photoshop.

Immediately after that there was another photo-op. Ken Sannison's role-playing fake woman, posed as Clint, and Millicent presented her with a NASCAR hat, signed by Kyle Busch. Another souvenir; an autographed picture of Will Ferrell, as "Ricky Bobby", standing with his arms around Clint Billson. This was the man that Candace had to face off against.

7

Face-Off

Hello, and welcome to the debate which will help decide who will represent the great state of Tennessee as Legislator in the House of Representatives. Will everyone please stand for our National Anthem.

"Oh, say can you seeeeeeeee...," the children's chorus, dressed in stars and stripes, wailed.

And now we will turn it over to our moderator, Clayton Cron:

Local newscaster Clayton Cron greeted everyone in attendance, live and watching from home, while both candidates strode out from backstage into a beautiful, royal blue-lit set with flags flapping and blowing in the breeze projected behind them.

"Good evening, everyone. I'm Clayton Cron, and welcome to our debate between the current State Governor, Candace Malone, and her opponent Clint Billson. This will be a debate focusing strictly on the issues of the nation and where the candidates stand on them."

Candace had planned to not shake the hand of her opponent to begin the debate, but when Billson extended his hand with a big, cheesy, white-toothed smile, she thought it would be better to return the smile and the shake. Candace wore a bright red dress, while Billson had the typical blue suit, white shirt, red tie, with a flag adorning the lapel. The applause trailed off, and Cron began, "The American people, and the people of Tennessee are a little fractured on some very important issues. Given your stances on guns, and gun restrictions, what compromises do you think can be made in order to bring people closer together?"

Candace shifted uncomfortably. She knew Billson's stance on gun restrictions aligned with what she truly believed, but she wasn't expecting the first question to be addressing this issue.

"Mr. Billson?"

Billson's alluring grin changed quickly to an expression of complete seriousness. "As you know, I am strongly in favor of gun restrictions. I feel that we as citizens have the right to guns as our Second Amendment states. But to be clear, the availability of guns—and types of guns which can be purchased by the types of people that have no right to have them in their hands alarms me. Now I'm not talking about those good, law-abiding folks here in this room, or in their living rooms watching tonight, but about the unlawful dregs of society that have no morality, no social compass, and kill innocent people just because they are unstable and have the ability to do so. I do not believe that guns kill people, but it's people that hold guns that kill people. So how do we determine the good and the bad? We can run background checks for psychiatric issues, or attend courses through our local good guys called 'police departments'. There is so much steps we are not doing, which is more important than taking guns away." Billson held his glare into the camera for a good few seconds then nodded in acknowledgment of the applause he was receiving.

"Governor Malone?"

"Mr. Billson believes things very different in life than I do. He believes in accountability, such as paying off a woman whom he impregnated." The crowd cheered, causing Candace to pause. "Well, then," she continued, "where were the background checks on Clint Billson's morality? Would they have helped? Would Billson still have done what he did? You see, Billson had an opportunity, just as an opportunity he is suggesting be mandated, but Clint, there are millions of other women, just as there are millions of bad people in the world, and you can't stop all of them, or in your case, can't even stop yourself. You can help by teaching right from wrong in schools. You can help by having mental health services available. Most of all, you can all help by not killing people—it is the individual's responsibility, and it is theirs to be accountable for not killing people. No one needs to remove guns from the rest of us!" The crowd erupted, clearly on Candace's side.

"A rebuttal, Mr. Billson?"

"Yes, I'd just like to say how I have owned up to my actions. In fact, Millicent and I have pretty much welcomed that woman and child into our own family. Yes, I made a mistake...."

"Humph," Candace interjected.

"I have made a mistake—"

Candace interrupted once more, "You sure have."

"But let me just respond with a few things about the gun issue, which Mrs. Malone certainly avoided. I own a gun, but I never have to pull it out...,"

"That's not what she says," Candace responded, a quick quip appeared virally on all social media, just about giving her election for State Representative, the next plateau in her political career. After this appearance, Candace Malone became not just a strong candidate, she became a political powerhouse.

Section 1, Part II

Peter

1
Backward

Once upon a time, in a place close to your home, at a perfectly average 7 pounds, 8 ounces, 19.7 inches in length, Peter Botchovich was born into a planet full of aliens. Not the outer-space kind, or individuals born in another country, but his feeling that everyone else in the world was non-human. He felt he was the human and everyone else was not at all like him. His mind continued to tell him that he was unique, but he was incorrect. It was only a feeling he had. In hindsight, *he* was the alien and the rest were just normal earthlings.

Peter was brought up by an emotionally cold but caring mother and an angry but loving father who only wanted him to do things an all-American son would do. The boy felt he was constantly forced into doing day-to-day normal things.

What did *he* want to do?

Peter had no idea what he wanted to do. Television was boring. Movies, conversations were the same. His father wanted him to participate in youth sports, but he wasn't blessed in that way. He was short and stocky. His father spent time with him to make him better, but this felt to Peter that he was being punished—the criticisms about things he was doing wrong, the open-fisted hits he would end up enduring. His mother, not the most creative or flexible person, didn't really know what to do so she didn't do anything. She would cook meals and straighten his room. She would complain about the state of it when she straightened. His mother would be thrust into silence if dad ever complained about the meals. This was not fairy tale. This once upon a time, was just a time.

So, the boy grew up in an odd way that boys usually don't have to grow up. He stayed in a tunnel which he created. It was such a long tunnel. It didn't end. When he got older, and graduated, he moved out—acquired a house as part of a pay-off, which he didn't want in some political move to silence him. *And his parents would live happily ever after.* His mind told him that too. The tunnel moved with him. There was some light far away at the end of it, but when he took a step forward the light moved away the same distance, and when he took a step back, the distance then increased. There was little brightness where he stood.

And the rain at night gave him nightmares. The wind in the trees along with their sounds gave him the feeling that the roof was going to fall in on him. He never slept on nights such as this because of the fear. It was a fear that fed his fear of everything. He always knew he was going to be a loner no matter what. That fear, the rain fear, the nightmares.

Peter never confessed that he killed animals as a child. It made the local paper though. Families missing their pets, and the bodies of those pets found in the woods. The chief of police said, "We are going to catch the sick individual who is torturing and killing animals in our community."

Peter once confessed to someone something else and ended up removed from his regular classroom. It wasn't about animals. When he was old enough to figure it out, he realized that most kids didn't think or feel the same way that he did. The soft conclusion from the experts was that he didn't adjust to things the way others adjusted. The harder, politically incorrect termed conclusion was that he was called 'bonkers', and thought to be just plain nuts by others. Nobody back then said words or phrases such as suffers with mental health, incorporating a suffix with the word disorder: anxiety disorders, panic disorder, obsessive-compulsive disorder, major depressive disorder, bipolar disorder, and other mood disorders. Let's not forget: eating disorders, personality disorders, post-traumatic stress disorder, psychotic disorders, including schizophrenia. Peter felt *bat-shit crazy*, so he learned to reel it in and to keep his mouth shut.

Peter was an outsider of the world. High school may have been his most successful time. Surprising to him and his father, he was on sports teams, but not a star, but still there was status in that, even if he wanted to hide from it. He had a girlfriend, whom he got pregnant. It was a sticky situation. He had to keep his mouth shut, but there was a break-up and a resentment, with so much inner sadness and anger. He never had or would have a successful relationship he treasured as much as her.

Then the boy became a man and had a job. Peter had some friends. Peter lost some jobs. Friends got lost too. People in society always attempt to harvest acceptance of people, places, and things. This man didn't. This man had trouble in that. Peter did not accept things, not just his negative progress, but where he fit or didn't fit in the world. It made him angry.

Peter also self-medicated, which is another word for

substance abuse disorder. You know that is a softer, gentler way to say what you really were known for. He thought, *Lucky. That's right. You are lucky to have gotten this far. You got through the good and the bad for most of your life. Things happen, don't they? For everything that happens there is an equal and opposite reaction.*

Ah, but this is only the beginning.

2

Hush Money

Peter defined himself as the person in what later would be called the "entanglement" with Candace Malone, then known as Taylor, back in high school. At the time, there wasn't the same shame for him that the Taylors seemed to be stuck on. He had a lot of pride that a girl like Candace Taylor, with everything going for her, would pick him to be with, pick him to have sex with, and strangely pick him to almost have a baby with. To Peter, this represented some sort of future.

What had bothered him the most, oddly, was not being responsible financially for the abortion her parents paid for, and their wanting to keep him and Candace apart. It hurt. Candace was his first everything. Somehow Candace validated his meaningful existence. Everything was better when she was around.

There was a large amount of hush money given to Peter by the Taylors, which helped cover it all up and erased the shame of getting her pregnant back when she was 15. Even back then, both she and her parents knew she would have a very public career. Candace Taylor, the future Candace Malone, the future powerful politician, would never even have existed if she had ended up with him, and everyone knew it.

The money Peter received was placed in a trust by the Taylors, and Peter would not have access to it until he was an adult. If Peter let the cat out of the bag, even to his parents, then he would never receive anything. It was enough money for Peter to feel fine with dropping out of college. He could always go back later, if he wanted, which is why he kept his word and kept his mouth shut. Then we Candace's career took off; Peter received an additional sum of money for an addition Non-Disclosure Agreement.

3
They're In The Trees

It was another night of Peter suffering the terror of the tree's branches scratching across the panes of his bedroom window in Chattanooga, Tennessee. As a child, when he slept in his parent's home in the village of Sentawee, he feared the same sound he was hearing now was that of a cold-blooded killer trying to get in to shoot him and then cut his body into a thousand ribbons with a hacksaw. This underlying fear never left him as an adult, whenever there was wind and rain at night, and even though he knew for a fact there was nothing to worry about, no one being out to get him, he couldn't get past the feeling. The thin twiggy parts scratched at the outside of his new house on Elm Street the same nails scratched on a blackboard.

It wasn't just the sound of the wind, or the tree on a window, or even the fear of being brutally murdered, that caused him to lie awake for hours during every rainstorm. It was the strength of his anxiety, a block of granite, that remained strong and heavy throughout his life. He'd lost a lot of hope in treating it, though he tried exercise, meditation, even a psychiatrist. Nothing seemed to help him, and now he lay here the same way he had hundreds and hundreds of times. Often this would accelerate to a full-fledged panic attack, which then made him completely give up on sleeping for the night.

There was a solution, not for his mental health, but for the tree. He had called several arborists, none of whom returned his calls. He concluded that they were holding out for the bigger job offers, and trimming a branch or two was a waste of their time. Maybe he could get them to cut down the tree entirely, but the roots and trunk were located over his property line. Nick Felton hadn't agreed to the trim or the elimination of his "mighty oak." Felton even wrongly labeled himself an arborist, when all he was trying to say was that he was a lover of trees and a lover of trees who wanted to keep all of the ones he owned, intact. Too bad he's not an actual arborist, one he could pay, Peter thought, as if this were true, all his trouble would be over, and the tree would be removed.

And then what? Things could go wrong at any time. There were people who went to work in the World Trade Towers one morning and never came back. People went to concerts or malls and ended up shot by a gunman who wanted to do something that the world could never figure out. People went for a drive and someone's brakes gave way, or a stop sign was ignored; perhaps the light turned red while someone sped through it, and BLAM-MO, life was over. Which is why, Peter stopped driving. Which is why, Peter eventually stopped working. Which is why Peter walked around as if he were wearing a vest with a bomb attached and some force of the universe had the detonator to *blow it all up*.

The perceived vest wasn't the only thing that made his upper torso heavy. Sometimes his thoughts made his heart heavy, and his lungs had trouble getting enough air. In an attempt to force the needed oxygen into his respiratory system, he accelerated all actions it took to breathe and ended up beaded with sweat, hyper-ventilating, with all of his senses inoperable. The symptoms of a full-fledged panic attack. He also would hallucinate ending up in various locations, waking up not knowing where he was, though often, he was in a church. The EMTs confirmed his panic attacks, but it seemed much less an attack than his day-to-day losing battle to overcome his angst. He was prescribed pills, and it was suggested he try meditation and prayer. He'd heard these suggestions before. Neither of them helped.

He wanted an answer. Was it his nature, or the way he was nurtured? His mother stored valium in the medicine closet because she was too anxious to drive all the way to the supermarket amongst other things. When he was a boy, it seemed his mother was preparing herself and the family for a long drive, one which took hours to complete, to purchase supplies that could last as long as possible. It was only much later, as an adult, when he went back to visit, that he realized that town was just a five-minute drive away from the house, and rather than the trek being the challenge, it was his mother that created that, it was she who created all her challenges. His mother was afraid of nature and not able to nurture.

There were other rules she had such as, "Don't walk by yourself," as doing that would be a risk of some unknown danger. The street they lived on had five houses, located in a rural area where the town's police blotter would document trash being dumped on someone's lawn as the main lead in the town paper. There were no violent crimes in the village of Sentawee. Still, Peter absorbed the fear, as if there were something in the shadows directly waiting to attack him. He was so anxious he would sprint up the street to decrease the possibility that *it* would.

It all seemed to come to a head when the large tree across the street from his childhood home was struck by lightning, and his mother's worrying about where it might fall caused Peter to be unable to sleep, the anxiety about being crushed far too great for him to reach a state of relaxation in which he could just drift away under the heavy, wool blankets and sheets. The sheets smelled fresh from being hung outside on the line, which should have caused Peter comfort. This was how the fear of trees in storms started.

❦ ❦ ❦

Nick Felton wondered what a person was doing on his front porch at such an hour, a person who lived next door to him and could come back at a decent hour. "Dear, God," Felton said, after answering the door, Peter on the front steps, short and stocky, face drenched by rain, which flattened his stringy, uncut, dark hair against his forehead. The water on his biceps made them look thick and full causing Felton slowly back away. Felton had not seen Peter very much recently. Peter's mother would still visit often and made sure to say hello. Felton thought she was very pleasant, but what was *this* visit all about in the middle of the night?

"What on earth are you doing here?" Felton asked. "Do you have any idea about what time it is?" Peter had an idea that it was after midnight.

"What would anyone possibly want at 2 AM?" Felton wailed.

"*Removal of your fucking tree, of course,*" was Peter's thought, but he only stood there and stared.

"Hunh??? What??? Please, no. You can't come in!" Peter hadn't asked to come in, so Felton's shaken defense, even though he was old and frail, seemed odd. Felton was confused, so Peter decided to enter Felton's house, just because he was unwanted. As he moved into the front hall area, he had the feeling he was being pulled into a tunnel of light, moving very quickly, his feet not touching the ground, heading toward some very bright pots and cast-iron pans circled in a horseshoe overhead in the kitchen. Peter's prevalent thought was to pull down one of the heavier skillets and bludgeon Felton, and then go outside to cut down the oak tree, letting it fall any place but on his house.

"You need to come back at another time!" Felton said, not as firmly as he wished.

Various words and phrases and answers to Felton's request popped into Peter's head, but nothing came out of his mouth. *Oh, the heavy...oh, the heavy* a strange repetitive thought overrode any potential thoughts about Felton's question, but Pete didn't say any words out loud. He gripped onto the marble countertop and knew that it was beginning this was it, and he was about to go under.

Then, Peter found himself being transported via a vision. The church's altar, adorned with gold leaf and crimson, the crucifix also gold as was Jesus. It swirled around, with a voice telling him that kindness was measured not within the act, but within the response to the act. Peter felt like the church was spinning. The pew felt like a roller coaster as Peter raised his arms at the crown of the peak.

When Peter was in this current blackout state, his feelings were almost completely opposite of how he felt immediately before he went under. When he came out of it into the harshness of what was real, there was a bombardment of distorted sounds, with his vision overcome by unforgiving light and a sense of smoke and fog. He could only compare it to the confusing moment of an auto accident, grasping at the disorientation, and piecing it all together as quickly as you could—the smoke being from the airbag deployed, the slow acceptance that the smoke was not the vehicle on fire. But what is next? Getting out of that car? Realizing that you are OK? But is everyone OK? What about the car? How long will it be before the police arrive? Immediately after an accident, your mind would piece it together in seconds, to come up with a plan on what you needed to do next.

In this state Peter still had thought processes, like dreams, except things were clear. He wished he could meditate and reach this same consciousness, having only peace and relaxation within. His mother stated she used to meditate, but to Peter it was just her on her knees praying, which he only knew because she intentionally left her bedroom door open. She also would say the rosary, which she explained to him as *reflective*. Peter never knew what she could possibly reflect on. Her life was so good. When she explained how it worked, he didn't see how anyone could reflect upon anything, except boredom within the redundancy of the rosary. And who ever thought of the layout of one bead, then three beads, then another one, before you reached the drudgery of five divided into sections of ten beads each by larger beads. It was like torture. His mother's was very ornate, fine pearly beads hung around a real wooden cross with a silver Jesus adorning that as well. If it was a more expensive rosary, it must be more powerful, Peter felt was her conclusion. He remembered a blue, plastic rosary he received at his confirmation, the beads having harsh seams, sharp enough to cut you while only a white string held it all together rather than a silver or gold chain.

This weak plastic rosary, the lowest form of one, was something which never worked for Peter, nor did any rosary for that matter. Rather than stick with something that didn't work, he gravitated to the other tool in his mother's toolbox which worked for her. He began to steal his mother's valium. Mostly, he would take it when no one was home, or when it was late at night so he could take as much as he wanted without being noticed. A few times the dose was strong enough for him to find himself waking on the hard wood floor, his face somehow melted partially into the polyurethane, with his saliva a gooey compound that held his thin lips like epoxy. Another time he came to in the middle of tossing half the food in the refrigerator down the garbage disposal. He became worried about all this after the last time, when he had killed a large dog. He came to standing over it, with no recollection. Lucky for him, witnesses said that the dog came at him and he had to defend himself. It was time to stop, which both Peter and his mother said they did. Instead, she just hid them.

After these episodes happened, in other moments of high anxiety, such as being in Felton's house, Peter would still enter a fugue state. It wasn't as cause and effect as taking 20-40 milligrams of a benzodiazepine, but it would happen without Peter having any control over it. His mother had learned to recognize it, and to talk him down and out, but after he moved, it was just Peter alone in the house, where nearly anything in the environment could prove to be a landmine. Something as innocuous as the thin branches of a tree scratching against a window pane, for a few nights in a row, would cause him to not sleep and easily slip into it. These factors made it easy for him to slip into the dark curtain and stay in that cordoned off area for various amounts of time. It was like the wind affected the branches, which set him off the way a Rube Goldberg machine works—one small push of energy starting a series of other events in which Peter would not awaken until the final yet spectacular ending.

On this night, when Peter's reality did return, he was being led out of Nick Felton's house by the police.

4

More on the Blackout Tunnel

How did Peter become Nick Felton's neighbor? When he was twenty-five, with the hush money he received he was able to afford a small two-story home on tree-lined Elm Street, in Chattanooga, and he even had some cash left over. The home was about ten miles from the village of Sentawee, where he grew up. He lived by himself, although he didn't want that. He would rather have ended up with Candace, if truth be told, and not have a house, except no one was allowed to tell the truth. Peter attempted to make the best of this lonely time, with not much contact except from the people he worked with. They filled the need for general people-existence and chit-chat, which reminded him it wasn't just him against the world; there were other people. Sometimes he went out with them for a few beers, just to feel like he existed...more chit-chat, more talking about the weather. It didn't actually matter that they were there, but it provided an excuse to not drink alone at home.

Often, though, when he was off work, he still felt alone. He got pretty good at masking those feelings, the ones of not fitting in, the ones of complete and utter social anxiety through which his behaviors often produced a loss of friends and the negative reinforce-ment of his worst thoughts. It made sense to him that he would enter his dark blackout tunnel. He never wanted to be in that place, that dark tunnel, which felt like the helpless place people have in certain dreams when you need to move quickly to protect yourself but your entire body is cemented there. There were so many elements spinning out of control in Peter's life and then suddenly they would stop, Peter finding himself within the tunnel. The blackness led him to be arrested for trespassing that night at Nick Fulton's, the court concluding that Peter was intoxicated and dangerous. Peter remembered nothing of that evening, which the court didn't agree with as a defense; they slapped a no-contact order on him and a weekly check-in with a court-assigned therapist, whose notes had to be submitted and reviewed by the court.

5

Therapissed

Peter's therapist, Kelly Granta, was an interesting choice by the court. She was young, tall, graceful, and came across as a kind soul who viewed her patients as stray animals, and of course she wanted to take them all in. She was a rescuer, but she was all in with giving the power to those she treated to rescue themselves. She knew that's how it worked. Even the coffee mug on her desk read, "I am not your Savior, Coffee IS!".

Kelly Granta didn't wear a business suit, but rather a white t-shirt and a variety of Free People colorful balloon pants. She clipped her hair in the back so the wide strand within it flowed like a waterfall. She could pull off being attractive wearing nearly anything, even a trash bag, unless it were full of trash. Kelly Granta had an immediate soft spot towards Peter but wasn't convinced that he blacked out during times of high anxiety. She was willing to listen though, as if it were true. *After all,* she thought, *isn't the main part of my job listening?* She was surprised that Peter was initially so open with her, but she thought it helped that her patient-client confidentiality allowed him to speak about Candace, her career, the gag order, and, of course, his anger and rejection. She wasn't sure he knew her notes had to be turned in to the court, and she didn't volunteer that information either.

It was difficult for Peter to talk about himself, even if Kelly Granta concluded how open he was potentially. Peter hadn't had too many conversations with anyone of late. What he should talk to Kelly Granta about was hard, having to do with loss, but whenever he tried, Kelly Granta would therapeutically push him for more information or acceptance. It made him uncomfortable, just as he might be if she told him he had to complete a triathlon right after they were done without training. He then avoided talking about anything conflictual, and he certainly didn't bring up how he harmed animals as a kid. That secret would go to his grave.

The sessions with Kelly Granta made him scratch at himself. When Kelly Granta pointed it out, Peter just responded that he needed moisturizer for dry skin. Peter was growing a beard, and beards are known to itch, so he needed to scratch at his. It was a good cover. He felt he was able to trick her by doing things like that, but she was on to him, just not pointing it out. The one time she did call him out on his beard scratching, he came in the next week clean-shaven. Peter certainly was not aligned with his treatment goals.

What were his goals? Kelly Granta had written that Peter was supposed to be working on joining social groups, attaining friends, and learning coping mechanisms, for his anxiety. His self-worth would increase if he succeeded in those things. As they continued to meet, Kelly Granta, realized she was hitting a dead end. She wanted to just fix him without his help, but recovery wasn't based on magic, so she couldn't spread magic dusk over him. *POOF, everything is better.* There was no fix for his abusive parents, and she concluded that he didn't know any other way or any other emotion but anger toward them. She wanted to bring up how and why he drank, which, of course, was connected, but Peter didn't see any relevance toward that. Basically, in his mind, he was the same person drunk or sober.

Peter did want Kelly Granta to be magic, then she could re-start him in high school. *Hadn't I been successful in high school? I was on teams, and I had dated the prettiest girl in the grade. I almost fit in, and things could have advanced, if only... if only... I could have done better and not been closed off. If only I had friends, and if only Candace or her parents had accepted me after all of that happened. I wouldn't have made all of these mistakes I have made in life. Things would be different, and I wouldn't be so fucked up right now, but I was never accepted then, and I still am not a part of the world.*

The reality of his treatment was, he was not hitting his goals and she was not magic, but for some reason, Peter kept having hope. The reason was he wanted to feel accepted and liked by Kelly Granta. Wanting to be liked was a chain around Peter's neck. It strangled him, and he felt like he was gasping for air in the presence of her. He soon realized that part of that was that she looked the way Candace did in many ways: Tall, high cheekbones, straight brown hair, and extremely put together, even when casually dressed.

Peter thought initially that Kelly Granta was young and naïve, though she was pretty good at her job. It was during his fourth session, only after he arrived drunk, that he brought up the relationship between him and Candace. It was difficult for Peter to mention any of it because it caused him to feel sad. angry, and to feel less than. He hoped Kelly Granta would get right on it and figure it all out for him. Peter just didn't have the courage. He downed a pint of bourbon in the parking lot of her office before each time they met.

If only Kelly Granta had a little more insight, that Peter revealing this kind of information was what most people would consider a breakthrough, but she didn't know Peter that well to conclude that. Also, Peter spoke to her in a very matter of fact way, as if he were reporting on the New York Stock Exchange. He dryly revealed that Candace was a woman of importance, and besides being the prettiest girl in school when they had dated, she was a known person in mainstream society today. Peter then said her full name, Candace Malone, but realized his mistake. When he looked up, and he noticed Kelly Granta nodding her head in robotic agreement, something in her closed eyes and body language hinting to him that she wasn't listening or didn't believe him. It felt like another betrayal.

His first instinct was to want to harm her. *She wasn't listening*, he thought. Then he had an epiphany. *It's perfectly fine if she isn't listening. There is no therapist-patient confidentiality here because her notes ARE to be collected by the court. It's better that I don't say anything of any value—anything I've ever done. There is no need to improve with her, no need to talk about killing animals as a kid or who Candace Malone was in my life Kelly Granta is no more than a paid service provide who doesn't give a shit.*

"Peter," she said. "we seem to have lost you right there. Focus with me."

The irony of her admission made him smirk. "I'm sorry, Doctor. What was I just talking about? I don't recall." He never did get around to discussing his true feelings around Candace Malone that day.

※ ※ ※

Peter was wrong. Kelly Granta had been listening. She was just tired, and Peter's tone was reminding her of the sound of her television right before falling asleep in front of it each night. She was an excellent therapist. She listened to everyone that she worked with. She also had a habit of listening with her eyes closed when she was tired, a trait that had been pointed out to her by her boyfriend. He too was a stray animal, not one ordered to talk to her, but rather someone who wanted to because he felt that she was his life partner. She wasn't completely sold on that idea, because stray animals are still stray animals, and their wounds are hard to heal, very often making them not solid life partners. She realized that this may be a repetitive pattern that wasn't very healthy, but she just couldn't seem to help herself. That afternoon she found herself typing in her notes: *Peter is like a feral cat with a wound which is very difficult to heal. There will always be a scar in that place, and it is a disfigurement to his psychological make-up which Peter needs to learn to not react to.*

6

Only If You Want It

Peter and Kelly Granta were at a standstill. Peter still physically checked in for his court-ordered therapy, and Kelly Granta attempted to keep things fresh and relevant but knew that Peter had already checked out. The sessions left her sad and frustrated. She wanted to help, and initially his shutting down made her try harder, but now she had given up. It had become obvious after he told her, "I'm only here because I have to be," but he still would perk up when she talked of hope, told him she saw his potential and that his life didn't have to be this way.

But it did. Peter couldn't see any potential. His fear and anxiety always put him in that same hopeless place over and over again. Having an attractive woman tell him he had potential was one thing, but having an attractive woman therapist say it, well, he thought, isn't that what she is supposed to do? It was paid hope. Life shouldn't be that way, but it was, and Peter believed that there wasn't too much he could do about it.

Theoretically, therapy works if the person believes change can happen and wants that change to happen.

Given those two things, Peter was in for about 50%. Change was stilted for Peter because the world wasn't in line to do that for him—it was against him. Anyone outside of his headspace could make an argument that this isn't true, but people, not just Peter, believe what they choose to believe, and once they believe it, then it is, to them, now fact. Therapy for Peter did something that was hard. It peeled back the part of the onion exposing the acceptance of the slow, dangerous, drudgery of life and straight to a quick, fuming boil about why life isn't what he wanted or expected it to be. The only acceptance he had, and continued to hold onto, was that he would never fit in.

So, today in session, Peter decided to call her out. It wasn't a slow and logical call-out, as now a wolf inside him had been let out, and Kelly Granta had stopped being a part of the solution. Kelly Granta was a part of the problem.

Peter's organic response to what to do with a problem was to eliminate it, which when mentioned in therapy sounded pretty good, except for one thing. Peter's response wasn't to solve the problem, but, to literally eliminate it. It created a serious conflict because Peter was still assigned to Kelly Granta. That eliminated the flight part of fight or flight. Peter could not eliminate her, the problem, without doing something he would regret. So, fighting to the death was out too. In this jail-like scenario, which he was sent literally to avoid jail, Peter decided just to serve the time until he could be let out. The time with Kelly Granta was not going to be put in as work which would fix him—just keep him out of jail. Peter put on his best face; nodded; said everything was great, and that he was making progress.

He was not.

Peter was still angry at the world and how he couldn't fit into it. The world needed to adjust to him and not the other way around. It, and everyone, was. out to get him. It wasn't a conspiracy if it was a reality, he reasoned. Look at the facts. Nick Felton was out to get him. The police were out to get him. Kelly Granta was out to get him. Even Candace Malone was...and of course, he didn't forget the wind and the rain out to get him for his entire life. Peter was a lone wolf trying to fight all of these powers that be. *I'm a fucking hero. I can make a difference*, he thought. *No one appreciates what I am fighting against*. Peter could also disappear into isolation, and none of these things would matter. After all, he had done that with his experience with Candace Malone. Suddenly, he blurted out while Kelly Granta was trying to talk to him about strategies he could adapt, 'Fuck, Candace Malone!" He had forgotten that Kelly Granta was even in the same room.

7
Rage, Fury, Wrath, and Irritation

It rained again that night. This was a problem for Peter because of his neighbor, and the tree, and the situation that Nick Felton had put him in. He had tried to resolve it civilly and cooperatively, but at 2 AM that didn't go well. He had dealt with things like this his entire life, and it had led him to right now, frozen in bed, with the twiggy outer branches of Nick Felton's tree going *scratch-scratch-scratch* against the panes of glass. In no time at all, it will be the heavy parts of the branches, followed by them breaking his bedroom window, ruining the house he bought thanks to his cooperation with the Taylor family. He knew it. It represented everything in his life. *Fuck, Candace Taylor AND her family*, he thought. *And fuck Nick Felton and Kelly Granta*. Peter reasoned, Candace did him wrong; Nick didn't allow relief from the tree causing him anxiety; and any hope he had of Kelly Granta helping him was gone.

The three of them were all of society and what society had done for Peter. People like them were the reason he was powerless toward unemployment. People like them were the reason he was powerless, period, and people like them were the reason he stayed frozen in bed during rainstorms. These people gave him nightmares he couldn't control. Sometimes he remembered his nightmares and sometimes he didn't, but even when he didn't, he woke with his cotton pajamas drenched in sweat, and the sensation that parts of his house had collapsed in one him. Fear and powerlessness were the worst thing in the universe.

Peter thoughts moved to the strategies he had tried to regain power. With Nick, he thought the last conversation about his tree should have succeeded, but the results of that was being arrested and being assigned to Kelly Granta. With Kelly Granta, anything he might have thought of as productive was erased by his perception of her indifference and boredom during their sessions.

Finally, with Candace Taylor, whom he refused to call Malone, he didn't need to do much. He believed that as a politician she will suffer enough. Peter took some joy out of her suffering, but most of the time he only felt the loss of her even as the years continued to slip by. He hated to admit it and would never admit to a secret that he held, one in which the house he had purchased with the Taylor's hush money would be a home he and Candace Taylor would share and spend the rest of their lives in. A big problem with that was that he had difficulty with what the truth was, which he was reminded of each time he checked up on her in the news. *Malone, Malone, Malone*, the name screaming out at him.

Malone? Christ, she would never be Malone, even if politically, they had plenty of common ideas. The big one was that she was Pro-Second Amendment, as was he. He had the right to be able to carry any gun he wished; it was a way to feel powerful and in control. Any little commonality brought Peter hope of him and Candace. Also, Peter joined the group *Guns for Nuns* mailing list, although he wasn't Catholic. He thought the group's name was amusing, and the red t-shirt he bought that had a group of nuns holding semi-automatics looked perfectly out of place when worn with his fatigue pants and cap. And just when the thoughts of guns and Candace seemed to lull Peter off to sleep, there was a sound as loud as a gun going off near his head, which made Peter leap up. He soon realized that there was no gun fire in his bedroom, just a large opening where the window frame used to be and a large branch of the completely fallen tree occupying his bedroom.

Section 1, Part III

Lucky

1

Prayers or Just Lucky

In a once-upon-a-town pulled from images of Norman Rockwell, a baby was born of a difficult pregnancy, which almost caused him, or the mother, or both to die. His tired, delirious father, Ted, said to his wife, "We are all so lucky he is here and alive."

"Lucky, then," Mrs. Waits responded.

"What?"

"Lucky, it is." With that, he had his name and a legacy.

To the Waits, he was a blessing, but they never considered how he actually zapped the luck out of them. Both of his parents wanted more children, but soon after, Theresa was told by her doctor that she and Ted could not have any more. The doctor said that Theresa had secondary infertility and couldn't get pregnant or carry a pregnancy after having the first baby. Both the quality and quantity of her eggs were said to be the cause. The Waits were also warned that even if they were to beat the odds, the chances of miscarriage increased greatly. Given the difficulty in their pregnancy with Lucky, followed by the current difficulty to conceive, and the risks therefore after, Ted and Theresa concluded that, yes, they had picked the perfect name.

But their boy actually was lucky, and his birth was only the beginning. His good fortune continued all through his childhood. The blond-haired child never lost at kid's games such as Candyland or Chutes and Ladders. The more chance involved, the more he seemed to beat the odds. When he was old enough to become a Little Leaguer, he wore number seven and caught anything he could reach. If it appeared he couldn't reach it, the wind would change, and the ball would die, and it just about fell into his glove on its own. Even when he was out of position the ball always found him. People were amazed how a boy who was not a very good athlete could excel in sports. He wasn't very graceful, but he remained unharmed if he fell down a long flight of stairs or off a roof. Both of those things happened in his teenage years. It became his own belief that he was blessed with luck, and that, not anything else, created his reality. He even pushed the limits, took risks because of it. A week after he feel off the roof, he attached a tightrope between the top of his parents' house to the adjacent telephone pole, and invited some friends over to watch him walk there and back. Lucky had never walked a highwire or even practiced the way tightrope artists train three feet off the ground, the way everyone was supposed to start. That day, when he was up there, high and mighty, his friends arrived, then looking up into the sun, saw the set-up, and begged him to come down. None of those pleas were heard as Lucky pushed inch-by-inch, foot-by-foot across, the taught wire with seeming ease. Nothing happens by accident. As some of us are blessed in glorious ways, and some of us are not. *I have been chosen,* he thought.

When Lucky and has parents were in a serious car accident it was still believed that luck was involved. Luck for him only. They were driving back from picking him up at college when he was asked if he wanted to switch off and drive. Lucky was tired and wanted to get some rest before he took over for a leg of a drive, so he said, "Give me an hour." He never saw what hit them.

Lucky was completely in a deep sleep when the semi-truck slid into their lane from the other direction. It was a long, slow arc around a turn from the opposite side of the highway, the centripetal force pulling the truck farther away from the side it should have stayed on. Research shows that people who are aware of an impending collision and have time to brace for impact have better long-term outcomes and less injury. So, why did his mother die and he live? Why did his father lose use of his legs and suffer from a head injury? Why was he, himself, unharmed?

The driver of the truck also had been asleep, just asleep, determined by the lack of alcohol tested for in his system. It was the size of his vehicle that managed to leave him unscathed as well. When the police came, both Lucky and the other driver tried in vain to get the family's car open, and to release the Waits, but the car was too damaged. Even the first responder highway officer didn't have the Jaws of Life. That arrived at the scene, but they had to call in for it. Neither of them could break through into the crushed front or side of the car, and pulling either of his parents through the back would be impossible. All Lucky and the truck driver had left to do was to walk close to the highway's shoulder while Ted and Theresa sat strapped in their crushed compartment as lifeless looking as crash-test dummies as the fire department worked to free them. Ted's legs were crushed. All Lucky wanted to do was to walk and walk and never return. In a way, that's exactly what he did. He left them, only talking about both his parents in the past tense, and never mentioning his father at all, unless it could be used honestly for some sort of advantage. For the people he would meet the rest of his life, he would only say that he no longer had parents.

※ ※ ※

It was during his junior year in college thatr he started studying business because he felt his calling was to be a stockbroker. He had the life experience of anything he picked working out, so why not make money on picking things which were guaranteed to work out for him financially? He wanted to work on Wall Street. He knew he could be successful there. Of course, one of his professors knew someone who knew someone and Lucky's path, as always, was all set.

It was also around this time he first started going to Atlantic City, wrestling with the idea of not continuing his studies, and just making money there the way he seemed to be. Yet, something held him back, even if logically both the stock market, and casino gambling would make him money. In the back of his mind was a fear, that something, he didn't know what, might happen at Atlantic City, where he could lose everything. Much like the tightrope, slipping was a possibility, not a probability, but this time he didn't want the possibility of falling hard.

Lucky always looked his best, and even casual, he could pull it off without trying. He was clean-shaven, wore his blond hair long, and wore bright-colored clothes, which often matched his bright blue eyes. He felt he was painted into the vibrant, explosive, colorful, life of Atlantic City, while everything else was sketched black and white. It was the place to be, for him, an important round hole phenomena for his round peg situation.

Even with that fear in the back of his mind about Atlantic City, he would still go and win. Why not? He won with dice, roulette, and if he ever needed an inside-draw for a straight in poker or the perfect card in blackjack, it always fell.

"Lucky bastard," he heard often at the poker table.

"Nah, just plain Lucky," he laughed. Others grumbled.

Pure luck was how he met Grace that night in Atlantic City, as he sat playing poker, according to those in the know, not a game of luck. It was coincidence that her father happened to be playing poker that night at the same table as he. They were away on a father-daughter trip, which he planned. Grace stood at the table as her father lost pot after pot to Lucky. Besides taking that money, Lucky was cleaning up that night, but Grace's father was the main victim. Not that Grace minded, because she silently was rooting against him.

Grace O'Halloran was one of the most striking women Lucky had ever seen. He played it cool, confident. Luck would prevail here too, as it did everywhere else. Of course, he was lucky at love too, but this seemed different. Grace was a total catch, thin, with strawberry blonde ringlets that wrapped around her ears, and cascaded down, floating down as light as the clouds that formed patterns as they moved across the sky. Her face was soft and fair, her eyes hypnotizing, and her social demeanor was along the lines of one-for-all, all-for-one. She was the blond, blue-eyed match for Lucky. She broke the concentration of every player at the table except Lucky. Lucky was too focused on how the time stopped when he glanced at her, while everything seemed to slow down, so he kept his head in the game. He wished his own presence at this exact moment would be doing the same thing to her, that he was the only thing that seemed to exist.

His angular and chiseled features, like the animated Gigantor robot, all hard right angles, squared like a Picasso painting, became filtered when he smiled at her and she noticed his face seem to soften. Although he was blond and blue-eyed, as she was, Grace sensed he was much darker. He had big hands, and a wide chest, with shoulders as hard as geometric rectangles. His eye contact was direct and purposeful—nothing lucky about any of his traits, because they didn't involve people, places, and things.

Grace saw her father catching the glances, and she shot him a stern look. To say the relationship between Grace and her father was contentious would be an understatement. He was not a present father at any time of her childhood. He drank. He gambled. He was often angry, and Grace never knew when that anger was going to explode.

And then he changed.

He went to AA and got sober, and found a Higher Power, and slowed down, according to him, his gambling. Grace still couldn't fully trust him. She knew that he had become a better man, and she even remembered times he was a good man when he was drinking or after being at the casino for days at a time. But you only get so much forgiveness for things done to you as a child in the hands of your father, even if he had stopped them, become religious, with some of his *isms* disappearing as if they never happened. She was skeptical, but she accepted that this was his way, and he was trying hard to come back into her life.

This father-daughter trip was supposed to mend some of the damage. He had paid for the entire trip, and even gave her a few extra thousand to gamble. Grace hadn't seen her father in years. She retained a good relationship with her mother, the person who made her the way she was... kind, empathetic, with a heart that knew how to forgive.

Now, here with a losing, agitated dad, the skin on her arms began to tingle, and she felt the top of her head beginning to sweat almost as if she had eaten hot food. She felt a panic-attack starting to grow, and all she wanted was to have that anxiety disappear. The parade of free drinks helped. She gripped the glasses tighter while her father ran his agitated fingers like a comb, back through his thinning blond hair. She wanted to be propelled out of the casino, feet off the ground by a high-powered wind, leave him forever, but like in the past, when around him she was cemented in place, this time over a poker table.

She needed to take control, take this power over her away from him. She made it a point to stand closer to the man schooling him at the poker table. When her father left the table, mumbling about 'going up to the room,' Grace was relieved. Then she replaced him at the table.

Lucky, the same way he did to her father, would take all her chips as well. He had a pair of kings dealt to him and she had two aces. The flop went nine of hearts, six of clubs, king of diamonds. He checked and she raised, and he called the raise. When a useless card fell on the river, the same pattern of betting occurred, but this time Lucky pushed it all-in, and took all her chips.

"Doesn't matter, he's going to take me to dinner," she told the dealer, loud enough so everyone at the table could hear.

Lucky smiled.

"You have taken enough of my money to buy me dinner, but I've drunk enough to probably say yes anyway," Grace said.

"More than enough," he added.

Lucky collected his chips and stood looking at her.

After a moment, he held out the crook of his arm as an invitation to take it. She did. They left the table together and headed out to the boardwalk; cool, salty air filled their lungs and they could both taste the ocean.

2
I Do

Lucky and Grace got married six months later, and she relocated to New Jersey. It was awkward having her father there too, but Grace was feeling a little better about him as the time passed. He was trying, still not perfect, but trying. In so many ways he was the opposite of Lucky, the vibe around him, though, indicated he had a past. This changed when he got sober. He had turned into a rather happy-go-lucky person most of the time, his personality having improved with the tools his recovery program laid out for him. Most of all, they now lived closer and he was back in her life.

Sometimes when her father was on a losing streak, he was on edge, which put Grace on edge. During those times, she set a boundary of leaving or telling him he needed to go to an AA meeting. It was exactly what he needed, and he would go without any reluctance, and come home in a much better state.

Lucky and Grace continued with their odd but strong connection. If Grace were to get honest, there was a part of this connection directly associated to her father that formed both the attraction to him and the old feeling of running away from her father. Even after their improved relationship, there was still a piece of her needing to flush her father away and to run so she could feel she had some control. A big problem Grace had was that this often came out as an acting-out behavior, which is why everything between her and her husband may have looked good on the outside, but on the inside, it felt like an odd relationship. Grace just hadn't figured it all out yet.

Grace's smile usually broke the tautness of Lucky's chiseled features whenever they were together. What Lucky also would find out, almost immediately, was that Grace was a giver, with an abundance of kindness for everyone. She forgave, proven with her and her father's relationship, and treated everyone as an equal. Grace told Lucky everything. In middle school, she once helped out a handicapped boy at the graduation ceremony, and the boy's parents praised her directly and to her parents. In high school, when she *was* one of the cool kids, she was able to hang out with every kid, even the handicapped boy. She was an unofficial guidance counselor for those who didn't have the confidence, or sometimes the support, of involved parents. And although Lucky presented to her as a winner, there was still a jaggedness around the edges that seemed to draw her to him. He was more than what her father first thought, that Lucky was just a way for her to get back at him. It wasn't that. It was more like the confident, independent Grace immediately felt she could pick Lucky. It made her feel edgy in a good way—first when this colorful man schooled her father. When she really thought about it, both of these relationships were extremely difficult to figure out.

On the other side of all of this was her mother, the person who walked her down the aisle. Her mother was the one who made Grace the person she was. Her mother taught her values of treating all others equally and kindly, and she lived that way for a long time, but her dad never applied those skills. Grace admired how her mother had thrown her father out years ago, because it was something she would have done if she could, but she had been just a child, too young to make that call.

Grace needed to be independent in all future relationships, and not being in control was not in the cards. Her first taste of freedom was when she left her home in Sunnyslope, Arizona, to attend college in Tennessee. Unlike many freshmen, she did not go hog-wild and party. She kept herself in check in order to focus on her future. She saw some of her classmates failing out and moving back home after the first or second semester. She also wanted to continue the persona of being The Nicest Girl in School that she had earned at Sunnyslope High School. She liked that and was very proud of being seen that way by others. After all, the world is a mean-as-hell place, and that could be found in every nook and cranny in every single, solitary location. The key was for her to stay in control of that by making her own decisions and making the right ones. She vowed to never allow herself to be dragged down ever again. When she didn't have that control, such as when she went back to Sunnyslope during school breaks, she felt anxious and almost defeated. *Learned Helplessness* led to apathy after being away. It was tough to go home, so she decided to stop.

※ ※ ※

At first, Grace loved the new life she and Lucky now had in New Jersey. She liked the cool underdog feeling Atlantic City had, and she enjoyed the many different types of people she ran into—all different sizes, shapes, and backgrounds. Her father spent more time at Caesars than with her, but that didn't bother her.

She also liked how her new husband could spin gold out of straw, because she was used to men turning everything to shit. How he was lucky at everything, was also fun, and at times, funny. In the early stages of their relationship, he didn't need to buy her gifts. Instead of buying flowers he would give her gems of banter. "You walrus hurt the one you love," he said to her when they were out at the aquarium, an example of his busted dam of puns he flooded her with. He also would sing to her every time they saw cows on their trips away from home, "Something in the way she moos, attracts me like no udder lover." Word play, coupled with his lucrative success at earning from his job, made her think he was a genius. They could now afford a house.

Their research led them to the place they would call home, Red Bank, New Jersey, an affluent area, and just about midway between Atlantic City and Wall Street. The place seemed wonderful. She and Lucky wouldn't have any problems affording the mortgage, as long as he continued to do unbelievably well at his job. His obscene success was unbelievable to people who had never met Lucky before, but it wasn't to Grace. He made it look so easy, but under the surface there was a lot of stress.

Grace felt some of her old anxiety rise up when his job was more intense. She chalked it up to "daddy issues," a term she despised. Lucky drank, but she still was made to feel more important than the drinks he needed to get past his stress. That never happened with her father. A lot of that Wall Street stress, Grace considered unnecessary, but it was part of the equation. One would think that being a stockbroker would be an easy slam dunk, for Lucky, given how everything always worked out, but it took a lot of diligence and a lot of hours for him to make money. When it did, the money always flowed.

All Grace wanted was things to be relaxing, free, and easy for both her and her husband. She started to get to know what was under the skin of the onion that began to reveal itself. When he felt under pressure, and suddenly needed to escape to Atlantic City, she took her trademark positive spin: that her guy was perfectly imperfect, and she accepted his imperfections. Lucky didn't see it that way. He needed everything to be perfect to reinforce everything that had ever happened in his life. His constant push for perfection, and the frequent trips to the casino, were the main things that worried Grace about their relationship. She would tell herself that it was all fine and that she was just reliving the trauma from her father. *This has nothing to do with her new life and marriage*, she told herself frequently. She always saw the best in everyone yet began to question his drive to be the best at something without any self-regulation. He didn't have to be perfect, but something had to give.

Atlantic City represented being able to breathe for Lucky. Instead of tight suits he wore at work, he could wear Hawaiian shirts. Instead of slicking back his blond hair, a look favored on Wall Street, his hair could be disheveled and wild. Instead of the social, controlled, drinking with the bosses, he could drink the way he wanted in Atlantic City. Grace enjoyed going there, at first, but it started to feel like she was watching a movie, the plot involving her father, her mother leaving the theater.

Lucky always left with more money than he came with, and often the slot machines he played would chime and flash from pot after pot. When Mr. O'Halloran was in town, Grace would stay home while her father often left with empty pockets and full of resentment of Lucky. He would continue to accumulate debt, and Lucky always lucky, would bail him out without telling Grace.

Grace knew something was up. She should have a resentment of one or both of them, or even feel disgust, but she stayed positive as long as her husband kept winning and her father losing everything was in order. She did not have to witness the father's serenity slowly disappearing after each dollar lost.

When she found out her husband was giving her father, because of his larger than stated losses, money, she was furious. She wasn't mad at Lucky, but at her father. Lucky bailing him out was on the surface not something which should overwhelm her, but it triggered her. She really tried to accept her father as a new man, but she couldn't look past this addiction—his need to gamble always more important than any relationship with any human being.

There was also a new feeling because of this. Her husband's luck, which had always thrilled Grace, started to annoy her, and resentment began to slip in. *How can things be so easy for him? How can this all make me feel bad, so without control? Why am I feeling bad? Why do I feel less than?* Logically, she knew being less than was not the case, but it got to the point she stopped going to the casino even when her father wasn't around. If he were winning, someone had to lose. Someone like her father. Someone like her. At home, she now refused to play friendly card games. Although she was pleasingly non-competitive, no one, not even her, wants to lose all the time—because that's not fun at all. She knew she wasn't unlucky at cards, but he was just so damn lucky. At least she could be lucky at love though, because isn't that the way the saying went?

Please, she thought. *Let me be.*

3
Ward Cleaver, I'm Not

Lucky and Grace could still be considered as having a good marriage, as for the most part, things worked out, some by work, but a lot by luck. Financially they were in good shape Lucky and Grace were both hard workers, and his extra element excelled in the earnings department. Also, superficially, they were attractive enough to turn heads on the street, causing the general population to riffle through their mental rolodex of celebrity couples to determine who exactly they were.

To Grace, though, Lucky's edginess, which was aligned to how he always got himself out of most jams in life, was unsettling. It was almost as if Grace were treading water with no boat, or raft, or life preserver in sight, but on the flipside, she wasn't getting tired and could seemingly stay afloat, without drowning, forever.

As long as she didn't panic.

When placed in dangerous situations, people who panic can lose both the physical and mental ability to survive. Grace didn't want to focus that she might be treading water forever, because if she did, she certainly would sink to the bottom of the ocean, her lungs screaming, trying to take in a deep breath of fresh air, while filling with salt water.

"Ward Cleaver, I'm not," Lucky told Grace when she felt things beginning to spin out of her control. "You married me for this...this away from the norm, and now you want it all dialed back? I'm not a go to work, deposit the check, pay the guy to build the white picket fence kind of guy. Never was." He looked out the window and saw the white picket fence which had been installed recently, and smiled.

"Maybe," she said, his smile still able to soften her. "I know it's what you do, and you do have that incredible extra element that everything always ends up OK, but I just have this feeling...."

"This feeling?"

"Yes, this feeling that one of these days it's all going to dry up. Lucky, I have a funny feeling that your luck can't always be conjured up to save you."

"I don't. It's just a part of me, so sort of, well, hard to describe, ummm, it feels like some sort of electro-magnetic phenomenon in my brain. I don't know, like how loaded dice work or magnets affect computer screens."

Grace felt a sharp tingle run down her spine, thinking that was a funny way to say it, after magnets around computer or television screens were not a good thing—they destroy them. And yet, he smiled, which melted her too. that Perhaps he could do no wrong, but suddenly she felt foolish. She felt she was being gaslighted by his good looks, his hypnotic smile. She knew he wasn't doing it to manipulate her. Lucky would never be accused of being slick or slimy, he just was who he was. *How could all this bullshit seem so genuine*, Grace thought, knowing that she wouldn't be happy with Ward Cleaver eventually either, even a drop-dead gorgeous Ward

Cleaver, but her intuition was strong. No matter how many times his attractiveness fought off her fears, she knew there was going to be a turning point, and both of them better be prepared and be able to adjust to it.

4
The Anniversary

It would be really easy for an outsider to rave about Lucky's life. In fact everything was so good about it, after a while, it would just be mundane.

This would change. It would become a story, starting with him and Grace having dinner in Atlantic City on their anniversary. Even though Grace felt anniversaries are more like an obligation than a genuine event, for some reason, she really wanted this to go well. She was starting to feel the distance in their relationship, which in the past meant boredom to her, but there was nothing about Lucky, as a human, that was boring, so she didn't quite know what to think. Mama Mott's was packed, which was not unusual. The host informed them the wait would be an hour. Lucky suggested they go to the bar. As they entered the bar area, they saw a couple get up from a table, and their name was called. "That's ours?" Grace asked, in a way which would indicate disbelief with most people, but she has been with Lucky long enough to know that these things just happen. Tables open up. They were seated with gleaming glasses, and silverware, and a crisp white tablecloth. "No line, no waiting at the bar once again," she laughed, enjoying him and his unique talent for the first time in a while.

"Oh, aren't you the lucky one now," he teased.

"You know, maybe tonight you'll get a little." A plate crashed to the floor.

"A little of what?" Lucky asked.

"Little dinner, little drinks," she said, playing with what was an obvious joke.

"How about we get lots of dinner and drinks. You said we were going to celebrate."

"Sounds even better. But I do want to go to the casino and recoup my losses from the market today, down again at closing. I don't usually win it back, unlike you!" Grace said.

"Inside information: The market always drops this time of year."

"Why don't you tell me *your* inside information then? You seem to do OK, even with a down market."

"Things work out." Lucky grinned, cunningly, like a cat that swallowed a canary.

"Maybe you can rig things the way you do. It'll keep our lives easy."

"Things are pretty easy now, but I try not to make it all automatic." He leaned over and whispered, "I'd rather not draw suspicion." He smiled and remembered what a solid pick he had made with her. To Grace, there was a flash remembrance of how things were when they first met. It had felt much different from anything she had ever known. In college, the boys Grace dated were all very similar to one another. Type A's, guaranteed to be successful, but even though they seemed to be on track with what she believed in, they bored her. With these types, it meant that she would be the one to act quickly and do the dumping so that there would be no chance that type boy would be the one to break up with her. No one would get the best of her, unless she let it happen, but once when she was caught off-guard it did. She felt completely defeated. *Damned fool,* she thought. *I will never let* that *happen again.*

She took that opportunity to hand-pick her next lover, one she couldn't possibly get hurt by. Clancy Tatem was the married professor of her Creative Writing class. He had been fairly successful as a writer, his topics heavy on alcohol and infidelity. The first time she seduced him was in his office. They had sex on his desk. All she could think about while this was happening was taking control and destroying something. "I hope you know, that this is separate, and won't influence your grade in any way," he puffed, out of breath.

"Shit," she laughed. "I did it for me, not for a grade."

"Listen," he stopped. "I have strings."

Grace glanced at the wedding photo pushed to the side of his desk by her ass, Clancy, standing with his new bride, looking about the same age as she was today. His dark features starkly contrasted her pale skin and blonde hair. "That married part doesn't bother me." Grace placed her mouth close to his ear and whispered, "As long as I get what I want."

"Well, whatever happens stays right here. Agreed?"

"Sure," she said, thinking, *This poor guy is in the wrong place at the wrong time.*

After the semester ended, they met for drinks most every week. She walked into their usual meeting place at the same bar, in a town twenty miles away, usually joining him in their same booth. Clancy was nervous every time they met, so part of the game was for Grace to loosen him up. She sat next to him on the same side of the booth, rather than across from him, so they both could see the comings and goings from the same point of view, and just in case someone walked in that he knew. After a few more vodka tonics, his fears were progressively removed, and his hands would find their way to Grace's legs.

After, they would leave the bar, often to the back seat of her car, without a second thought. Hours later, when he arrived home, he would tell his wife, "Work took me longer than I thought, and traffic was hell," the excuses seeming tired even to him.

The next time she and the professor met, she told him how bored she was becoming, and that this would have to end. He looked down sadly at the wooden table in their booth. "Damn," he said. "What about us? I took quite a risk doing this with you."

"Us?" She let out a hardy laugh. "I never told you that this was going to amount to an us," she said with calculation. "What it amounts to...," Grace said motioning her arms around the booth like an orchestra conductor. "This."

"I thought we were starting something pretty good," Clancy said.

"Let me go through this with you. You are the married one. What were you really going to do? Sorry to burst your bubble here."

"I would... I would," he said, fumbling.

"You would do nothing, because that's what men do," she said without restraint.

They finished their drinks and didn't end up going any further that night or ever again. Grace had won. Grace was relieved that it was all wrapped up and she didn't have to be do it anymore. Her plan had worked, and her life was unaffected until a few years later when his book *The Professor of Love* became a best seller, and she was the main source of material. *I'm living a life of fiction,* she immediately thought.

5
The Turning Point

Grace turned to Lucky, as she forked a piece of tiramisu. "You don't write, do you?"

"Hunh? Where is this coming from?" he asked.

"Thank God! I dated a writer four years ago, ended up in his book."

"I think I'd like to read that," Lucky said.

"Let me put it to you this way. Did you ever read *The Professor of Love?*"

"No, but I saw the movie," he answered.

"Well, the Nastassja Kinski character was based on me, sort of," Grace said.

"Wow. You were kind of a bitch! I mean, in the movie."

"Well, there are two sides to every story. He wrote his side," she said.

"But, of course, you were hot," he paused, amused with the lunacy of how someone's life can be displayed in a book or on a screen.

"But it's probably pretty true, right? I *was* a bitch. I really used him," she reflected. "Casting Robert Redford was a mistake. I mean, he's blond. Didn't look at all like my professor. I was the blond one."

"You could have done worse", Lucky said.

"Too many pock marks." Grace wanted to change the subject, "I'm stuffed. The veal was tremendous. I would like another drink though. Let's have one back at The Resorts. They'll be free there."

Lucky ran to hold the front door for her, half-stumbling, slightly drunk, exaggerating his role as a gentleman for comedic effect. Then he grabbed her hand for the walk up the boardwalk. It was the only thing besides the scotch that gave him warmth this evening, the ocean breeze creating a damp and cold environment. "Ooh, look at the moon," she remarked, at the very bright full moon present. "See how it lights the sand and the sea."

"Sure does. Everything's all lit up," Lucky agreed.

"I wish it could warm things up. It's so cold." she shivered.

He removed his hand from hers and wrapped his arm around her waist, pressing her hips against his. "Is that better?"

"Better. It's like a nice brandy. When we get there, let's play something together. What do you feel like playing?" Grace asked.

"I don't know yet. I feel what to play when I see it. Usually, my first impulse rings pretty true."

"And what was your first impression of me? The first time you saw me at the poker table?" Grace asked.

"Pretty. Your face seemed to be glowing. I knew I would kick your ass in poker, after kicking your dad's, but somehow, I also knew that we were going to end up together."

"I was hoping more along the lines of, 'I wonder if I have even a chance with her. She's out of my league. And for the record, I didn't mind losing to you in poker," she said.

The lights from the Resorts cut through the

darkness, overpowering everything, even the moon. It was a way to attract people in this very competitive gambling market. Some offered free bus trips and extra chips, while others offered even more—meals, rooms and whatever they could throw at the high rollers. All of them seemed to have free drinks and none of them had clocks. The Resorts Casino had its own gimmick. It had a "Spin to Win" slot machine. When you entered, you were allowed one spin on the special slot for a chance to win a big payoff and various prizes. Usually, you won game credits, or steak dinners, which you couldn't cash in. Grace entered the Resorts before Lucky and had the first spin—and came up on "FREE DRINK."

"Ha!" she exclaimed. "No one wins anything, except the free drinks you normally get anyway."

Lucky took his turn. He pulled down hard and waited to press the stop button— "BOARDWALK-BOARD-WALK-BOARDWALK," the machine read. Sirens went off; strobes blinked; and lights spun. Lucky's white shirt was bathed in red and blue light.

"A WINNER!" the host yelled. "You won a trip to our sister casino, the Resorts Casino in Vegas!" The white strobe lights drew Lucky into them, and they seemed to burn deep behind his eyeballs. He had the weird sensation, which he would describe later, that everything appeared to be buzzing. The sound increased, and was increasingly distorted, synchronized with the lights. The red, the blue, and the white lights, spinning and flashing. The white ones were causing him to wobble. To him, the lights were going off again, in the past that would have indicated that Lucky was a big winner...for the second, third or fourth time in a row. Instead, something else had happened. He imagined himself all alone, but not just from Grace. He imagined himself alone and walking, looking at sheer panic, and sensing people being in danger. Then, he went down like a sack of potatoes. Then twisting and shaking on the ground, producing garbled screams for over five minutes. When he woke up from his seizure, as if he were emerging from a blackout, he forgot how grateful he had been just an hour or so ago.

6
Lucky?

Lucky had had a Gran-Mal seizure, which seemed to have been brought on by the strobing whirlwind of lights and sounds at the casino. The doctors in the ER couldn't narrow down exactly what happened, which is why at times they hypothesized, but after they ran an EEG, which concluded a deficit, they released him, because he refused to even want to receive the information. He also refused further tests. He told them that everything was fine.

Two days later, his doctor, Dr. Kim called, and Lucky didn't pick up on the first call. He knew it was going to be a "this was a one-time event, and you're lucky to be alive...nothing to worry about" prognosis. Instead, Lucky, listening to the voicemail later in the day, was informed that the EEG was abnormal and he should come in to discuss options. Was he free tomorrow?

"You really should," Grace, the practical one in the relationship, said.

"I'm sure Dr. Kim just wants to be paid for the visit," he replied. "I'm fine."

Grace, knew better than to doubt him, because conclusively things tended to go Lucky's way even if the odds said that they shouldn't. The following weekend, Lucky had another seizure while in a car wash.

"Stress?" he asked Dr. Kim.

"We found some lesions," she said.

"Lesions?" Lucky asked.

"Yes, lesions on the brain," she added. Grace reached over to grab his hand, and Lucky threw her off like a dog shaking water off his coat. "The news may sound bad, which is, you are likely to have more seizures," Dr. Kim explained.

"Sound bad?' Grace responded, as Lucky shot her a 'be quiet' look.

"The good news is that with less stress, and definitely less alcohol, the lesions should heal to the extent that the seizures may be very few and far between."

"But my job?" Lucky asked. "Do I have to quit my job?"

"That depends on if you can work with less stress around that particular job...so, no, you don't have to leave it," she said, then quickly added, "but you should definitely quit drinking. If the lesions weren't caused by the drinking, they will become more pronounced by it in the future."

"I can do that," he said in a non-convincing way, almost spoken like a question, causing Grace's head to volley back and forth to the faces of Lucky and Dr. Kim, looking for some help, or perhaps a mandate, which would never come.

"If I have to," Lucky then said.

※ ※ ※

Lucky got home and poured himself a drink, causing Grace to want to blow her top, but holding it all back, not to upset him and perhaps cause another seizure. Lucky caught her look and smiled.

"Don't worry, baby," he said. "These things will work out for me. I'm not planning to change anything. Let's see what happens."

"Why do you treat your life like it is some kind of roulette wheel?" she shot back.

"Well, you know me pretty well, but not for all my life. You'll see exactly how this will work out," Lucky said.

"Wasn't very amazing, what happened to you?"

"Well, maybe without my luck I might not be standing here."

Grace ,who always imagined a partner with a positive outline on life, could not get behind Lucky's version of his glass being half full, or, in his eyes, completely full. Today his glass seemed to be spilling, the wrong direction to be heading.

"'Round and 'round we go," she said.

And where it stopped was between the ER and multiple medication changes. Lucky hadn't stopped doing anything, so the seizures stayed active. These repeated seizures kept Lucky in a very vulnerable position. He did not like to be vulnerable, because he had no experience with vulnerability. He was not used to things no longer working out, because he had always seemed to pull things from out, seemingly out of his ass, to make them work. On the way to his new neurologist, he had a small seizure, remained aware enough to know he was unable to control his car, and smashed into the vehicle stopped twenty yards from the spot he started to have his medical issue. It was another trip to the Emergency Room, with a new recommended round of medication, which needed to be followed up with at his next neurology appointment.

The latest medication, Depakote made him groggy, which he didn't like, and for which he blamed his latest losses in Atlantic City. But it wasn't because he was tired that he didn't get the cards he usually got. Two-pairs stayed two-pairs and never became full houses. He blamed his lack of luck on the seizures, the medication, his job, his wife, in fact, anything but luck or he, himself. Grace became increasingly aware that he now drank even more than usual, and she didn't enjoy how the increased alcohol seemed to increase the release of his frustration, often taken out on her, and sometimes on objects. At work, when she told a co-worker he was no longer happy-go-lucky, a colleague named Michelle, dryly added, "Sounds like he's become happy-go-abusive." Grace stopped talking with her and was not ready to commit to Lucky being what she said he was or to admit to others, what might become be a long-term issue. Not yet.

Grace tried to approach him from different angles, getting him out of his funk, but each time without success. Quickly, she gave up on the medical argument that the alcohol and Depakote were a bad mixture for the ability to function and control seizures. None of this seemed to make much of an impact, because Lucky felt that none of it was going to be a long-term problem and that things were going to work out for him the way they always did. Plus, Lucky did his best to tune out her messages, because, why bother.

They both waited, him for improvement, and her for him to improve, but things didn't get any better. Grace even stopped discussing having children because he didn't seem to be able to control his moods from one day, one hour, one moment to the next. She didn't want to have kids with that kind of turbulence hanging around. He became the child who needed to gain control, because he had lost nearly all of it, and the progression from being fortunate to not having any luck at all was worsening. Grace was keeping more and more of a distance. She had started to question what the use of her being there for his best interest was if he was completely uninterested in listening to her.

While Lucky's impatience caused increased agitation, Grace tasked herself less with helping him, more with documenting outbursts to potentially use later. She started a notebook of all the times he presented anger, not just toward her, but toward various pieces of furniture, walls, and appliances. He also was becoming less patient. When he could not stream programs he wanted to watch because the WiFi went down, he slid his fingers under the base of his MacPro and flung it high up to the ceiling, the laptop crashing down shattered and tousled like a dead bird falling from the sky. Grace, always upbeat and confident, had given up. She was scared. She didn't show it and didn't cower, because Grace never would cower. Ever.

Grace then made a move. She apologized to her coworker and started to sit with her at lunch. She found out a lot about Michelle during these times, as Michelle began to open up about her own past and how she left a relationship which was just as volatile as the one Grace was currently experiencing.

"Will he agree to counseling?" Michelle asked.

"Marriage counseling? I doubt...."

"No, just for him. The marriage is broken and he has the key to fix it, not you and him together. It's him. It's up to him to do this. Plus, if it's not going to work out, then counseling will start leaning you toward how you can live without him."

"I don't think I love him anymore," Grace said, realizing she had the ability to take control of her situation the way she had done for her entire life.

7

Bingo

Bingo's Bing-Bang Gun Shoppe was a perfectly good gun shop with perfectly good waiting periods, which covered perfectly good background checks. But if you were in a pinch, needed something right away, and you were willing to use the code-word 'Bazooka', and had an extra $5,000 to $10,000 dollars to give Bingo, then you could walk in and out with any gun you wanted, no permit required. That was the word on the street anyway, because those folks knew that Bingo's needed to be competitive with street sales, as on the street you could buy any gun you wanted just by meeting up with the contact person, usually, himself, armed and dangerous.

Lucky found that to live in a house with someone you love that no longer loves you is the same as being underdressed in a drafty home. It's cold, doesn't warm up, and there is a constant reminder of the discomfort. Grace continued to do her best, not showing her cards, but she was broken inside. It was Lucky who was more emotional, but not in the way of sadness, or even his recent anger. He had stopped shaving and spent a lot of time in the spare room of the house. Even disheveled, he remained handsome the way a Hollywood actor playing the part of a down-and-outer, couldn't quite pull it off.

He also had quit his job. He blamed the extra stress the job caused for triggering his medical condition, and he would recover financially based on his upcoming rash of luck which would undoubtedly occur. Mostly, he just didn't feel like working anymore. Grace sarcastically told him the other day that, "You should go out and meet someone, it would get you out of the house." That just made him want to stay home even more, living in the pain when all he wanted was for it to end, and then things could go back to *normal*.

Lucky fantasized about the quickest way to solve the problem of the pain caused by Grace. He briefly thought about going to Bingo's Bing-Bang Gun Shoppe, buying a gun, and killing her, but that thought quickly diminished. Then he thought about killing himself, and that one stuck with him a little bit longer than the previous one, but that too eventually left him. Lastly, he thought about going hunting and killing deer, or something he could kill and then eat, then he would have an excuse to kill something.

His last thought was to get a dog that would hunt with him, so he decided to get a dog first, then maybe Bingo's on the way home for the gun. He had to make a visit to a very bleak looking animal shelter, which was a kill shelter. Dogs were piled upon dogs, in cages, amongst incessant barking and shitting. Lucky could smell the place while walking ten feet from the front door, and then, upon his entering, the smell overloaded his receptors, sending a wave of nausea and disgust through his body. Everything bad having to do with dogs and dog shelters forced him out of there after fifteen minutes. He could look at the dogs they had online and come back to the shelter only to pick up his new dog, or so he thought.

Even after he left today, without a dog, he couldn't get the sounds and smells out of his system, every breath of fresh air smelling of shit, every sound a loud echoing bark. He feared that these might produce another seizure.

The next day he went back because he saw online that a yellow lab was available, so he called to make sure he didn't have to wait and sit in the smell, but they told him he'd better get there quick. Yellow labs get snatched up, and his wasn't the only inquiry. In kill shelters these breeds were rare; the dogs all tended to be, more often than not, American pitbull terrriers or derivations of them promoted as dogs of another breed. Yellow, chocolate, and black labs came in all pitbull varieties. Scrunching his nose, he entered, almost running, in an attempt to outrace the smell. A woman in front of him, slightly average in every way, was asking about the same dog, *his* dog. Her hair was curly, and when she turned upon his, "Hey, wait a minute!" the locks bounced softly upon her shoulder like a small jaunty wave in a warm green ocean. He stopped, his directive swallowed by her piercing, then softening, eyes.

Quieted, he said, "Hey, wait a minute. You got here just a minute before me...you must be lucky."

"Lucky?" she repeated, and, phrase that normally he would respond to with a swaggered, "Yes, that's me," was only replaced by a nod, as today was just another day in his downward trend, and it didn't feel lucky to him at all. The dog would be hers.

"That's my name," he said, barely over the sound of one hundred dogs.

"Lucky?" she said loudly, motioning her head toward

the back kennel. "Your name is Lucky? These dogs are the lucky ones. Here. Take dibs on mine. I'll adopt another. There are plenty of dogs here."

She took a step into the stench of the kennel, directing the handler holding her yellow lab to give it to Lucky; the thin, panting dog no longer was hers. Immediately, names popped into Lucky's head, Bingo for the dog and Abby for the woman. He didn't have to ask Abby; he already knew he had her name right and felt a swell of relief knowing that things were getting back on track. His luck had changed momentum, and it was Abby relieving him of his slump. None of it had anything to do with him...the good or the bad. It must have been all about Grace zapping him of his strength, causing bad things to happen. *It was his situation*, he reasoned. Grace had some part of being at fault. Grace had neutralized him, which clarified everything. All in all, that was the perfect explanation, because it allowed Lucky to once more have no accountability.

When Abby came out with her potential dog, he called out to her by name, which should have surprised her, but somehow it didn't. Her head shot up from the dog on her leash to him, her eyes like full moons, blinking mechanically. They appeared to be like a winning slot machine, and Lucky hoped he wouldn't seize like he had that time the bells and whistles of the casino caused one. It did not happen, and the two of them held a look of wonder and curiosity in each other's eyes. Then he said, "Abby, let's take them around the building for a walk."

"Did you...could you have...how did you know my name? Did they mention at the desk?" finally realizing that he had pulled her name out of thin air.

"No, it just came to me. Sometimes things like that just happen with me," Lucky explained.

"Umm, OK." she said.

"So, walk?"

"Umm."

"You don't have to, but I think...," Lucky began.

"OK. Let's walk and see if the dogs get along."

8

Home Game

Abby Shipp's chosen dog was a gray and white pit bull she named Manny because of her affinity for the Boston Red Sox, having grown up on the island of Nahant, which was, in fact, not an island, but rather a tombolo; effectively a peninsula. Folks just said island because saying Tombolo of Nahant was just an awkward thing.

When Manny got into mischief, Abby said, he was just "Manny being Manny," which allowed great tolerance for the new human. Lucky was just, "Lucky being Lucky." In the presence of Abby, he was just starting to get his luck back, slightly, at a slightly above average level.

Abby liked him being around. Abby originally had moved to New Jersey from New England with Jack, who thought the move would be a perfect way to run from her less than perfect family. But after a few months, Abby decided to run from Jack as well, and when he left, he took their three dogs, Big Papi, Nomar, and Kennedy.

"Yes," she said, shifting on her purple sofa, after their weekly walk around the dog park. "Kennedy *is* a Red

Sox name, not that you'd have heard of Kevin Kennedy. People always think he was named after JFK."

"Why did you stay here? Why didn't you return to Boston?" Lucky asked, as she handed him a drink.

"Because then I would lose. I didn't want to feel like I had lost. I wanted to feel like moving here was a decision I had made, and I want to make it work. Plus, I have a lot of support here. There's a grieving group I attend weekly, which really helps."

"A relationship grieving group?"

"No, not exactly. It is a bereavement group, but I pretend Jack had died. It almost feels that way to me. No one asks me for a death certificate."

Lucky laughed and again was driven into her eyes, which were bright and gleaming the way shiny crystal reflected the light of a brightly lit room. He wasn't sure if it was their natural state, or if the conversation had caused her to mist up a little. Lucky paused the thought and wondered if he too should go to that group, but then he quickly dismissed it because he and Grace were still legally together and Grace had not flat out asked for a divorce. It was probably on the way, but he didn't want to explain to Abby that he was married. It was a fact he'd rather not get into at the moment. Instead, he pushed her soft brown curls back from her neck, touching her skin with his fingers. Abby's hair responding the way Grace's no longer did, Grace's curls to him felt hard and crusty. *I no longer have this with Grace* he thought, justifying his action. He reasoned that just when he needed her the most, Grace had deserted him, which might have been the case except for one thing.

❦ ❦ ❦

When Lucky returned from Abby's house with his dog, Grace had no idea about where he had been or had ever heard of anyone named Abby, but was ready to rip into him.

"Don't you see that you are acting out!" Grace said pointing to Bingo. "You are acting out because things just aren't going your way. Why don't you talk about it instead of all of these mini-tantrums and dog purchases!"

"I am. I'm telling you that I'm frustrated. I'm frustrated with everything and especially how you've changed, and how it's affecting me...my life...seizures...."

"How I've changed? Me!" Grace shouted. "As if I've caused this! Do you have any idea? Do you have any fucking idea how different you have become? You come home drunk today, no surprise, and with, with that dog! You never asked me about getting a dog." Grace's anger surprised her, as rarely had she allowed herself this.

"I didn't have to, and her name is Bingo, by the way" he said, while thinking, *Bingo is my dog, not ours is why I didn't ask, so there's that. Anyway, there is more of a connection to the dog with Abby, so there's that. Anyway, there is more of a connection to the dog than a connection to you, so there's that. And, if Grace only knew of the alternative, that I had thought of killing her, she'd be overjoyed that there was a dog in the house. The dog had saved her life. There's that.*

"You damn well should have asked!" Grace responded.

"Not if I decided to hunt. I don't need permission to hunt," Lucky asserted.

"Hunt? What does...?" She stopped. "You don't fucking hunt! Hunt what??"

"I was planning to start. I don't know, deer, pheasant, pigs?"

"You were going to hunt fucking pigs?" Grace shrieked.

"I don't...," he said, trailing off.

And then Grace got an image of Lucky, out on a farm in fall hunting gear hunting pigs, and she spit out the drink she had just filled her mouth with and laughed until her eyes filled with tears, while Lucky looked at her as if she were crazy.

❦ ❦ ❦

The rain would start any minute, and it was looking to be a good one. The clouds had started to change from a washed out grey to a flat black, and the wind caused the tree's branches to react stiffly, their arms robotically jutting up and down. Their dogs circled one another, off leash, in the open field—the friends playing like they've done since Lucky and Abby began their weekly walks.

"Manny is going to need a valium," Abby said, looking at the sky, her red and white patterned dress pinned by the wind against her legs, pushing up against her thighs. "He gets terrified from thunder storms. Must have had a bad association with them."

"I think I'm going to need a valium," Lucky replied, and Abby didn't laugh, so he changed direction. "We should head home then," he added as Bingo panted happily, showing the emotional range yellow Labradors have at any and all times. There could be an atomic wave from a nuclear bomb detonating and a yellow Lab would be making friends.

Abby quickly clipped Manny onto a leash and walked rapidly in the direction of her house, about a five-minute walk. Lucky's car was at Abby's house. He followed without restraining Bingo, so she walked up people's driveways and onto their porches.

"Come on, hurry up," Abby pleaded, growing impatient with both of them, as the sky flickered.

"Oh, she's just trying to make friends...maybe get a handout. She knows the houses. Everyone in the neighborhood is getting to know her," Lucky said.

"Hurry," Abby repeated. "I'm not going to have time

to get his medicine into him so it has time enough to work." The lightness outside was dimming as if God were sitting in front of a giant wall switch, his deft fingers turning everything progressively darker. Now that was a ridiculous thought, Abby realized. First of all, she didn't believe in the "man in the sky" version of God, and second, why would he be controlling everything like a light-person at the theater.

They were only a minute from Abby's when the sky opened, the moisture weighting down her curly corkscrews until her hair flattened. They held hands as they walked quickly in tandem, almost running, with the dogs as their escort. When they reached her front door, they were soaked, their breathing causing their chests to fill then deflate. Abby fumbled for her keys, and Lucky was close enough to feel her warmth radiate through her wet clothes. He gently pushed her up against the wood door, their wet faces and lips making hard contact, and before locking into place, random to focused. She turned from him, the key engaging in the lock with little resistance, until it was firmly in, ready to be turned, the metal lock mechanism making a popping sound. She was silent as she stepped into the kitchen, and quickly grabbed a slice of deli-meat, rolled it around a 5mg Ativan, and fed it to Manny. She continued down the hall past the living room, into the bedroom, Lucky, and Manny right behind her instinctually, no words needed. Hair dripping, she sat on the bed for a few seconds until Lucky pushed her down with kisses, flanking her, his right hand now pulling up her dress from being flat on her mid-thighs to resting over her stomach, revealing custom-fitting cotton panties that lay over her like they were formed to her shape.

Lucky slid his finger against the elastic, removing the garment and pulled their torsos together with his arm, kissing her soft twice, and then a more prolonged kiss, similar to the one in the doorway. Their lips continued to push against each other, as Abby, at times, disengaged pulling on his bottom lip between hers. Lucky, after unbuttoning the back of her dress, continued to work her with his hand, teasing with the touch firm, then gentle, until her body rose up, physically indicating what she preferred.

Abby's face and bare legs flashed from the storm, even with the shades pulled down, as the lightning strobed for them. As he kissed her nipple, he entered her with his finger, working it through the tense contractions, until suddenly it loosened, and Abby, breathing hard, exhaled quickly four times, a prelude of voicing before she became undone.

✺ ✺ ✺

Manny was asleep in his dog bed in the right corner of the room, past the foot of the bed. Abby's head rested on the crook of Lucky's shoulder as they lay silently.

"Was that alright?" he asked.

"Are you kidding me?" Abby said.

"I just wanted to make sure."

"You couldn't tell?"

"It's important that it was good for you. I can get off on my own anytime."

Hearing him say, *get off*, made Abby lift her head off the nook of his shoulder. She felt her body beginning to tense up and his features looked more chiseled than they did in the flashing lights. She wanted him again. "Don't worry about it," she said, getting up. "It was good."

9

Sump Pump

The heavy rain caused the sump pump to audibly make a whirring sound, vibrating the house for about ten seconds before it shut off. Grace had Lucky install it the first time the basement flooded, when they were standing shin-deep in the brackish water with a Shop-Vac, praying a plugged-in lamp was not going to fall into the water and kill them.

When this all ends, she thought, *every time it fucking rains, I'm going to be reminded of him, for ten fucking seconds at a time every five minutes or so.* She wasn't sure of what she was feeling, as her anger was still mixed with some pinches of sadness, but she wasn't even sure if she ever wanted him to return. She knew she would only be angry when he did return, but also sad if he didn't. His drinking had started to remind her of her father, and she knew how that story played out. *I've allowed men to control how I feel, and to produce feelings. Men have made them not what I want them to be, just because they have existed*, she thought. *I hope he doesn't come home, or maybe, better, he was struck by lightning.* Then she worried that the flashing lights may have caused a seizure and he was out there lying in a puddle, with that stupid dog barking away, and she felt like an uncaring bitch, suddenly angry not at him, but at herself. Then the sump-pump went off, and it would go off thirty more times before he finally came home.

He smelled minty. Lucky had unwrapped a toothbrush from Abby's supply closet and brushed her taste away. He also left it in the cup next to her sink, to use for the next time, and then soaped up his face, because smelling like toothpaste and soap would have to be explained less than smelling of someone else.

10

Moving

Lucky was gone more often and returned each time smelling like toothpaste and new soap. Sometimes he smelled like other things. It didn't take a rocket scientist, or even a fifth-grader for Grace to put two and two together. She had her things in order. She had the notebook, the name of a good therapist, and the name of a good lawyer. Each of them advised her that the process would be smoother because there were no children involved. Grace did invite Lucky to see the therapist with her as a last-ditch Hail Mary, to see if there was a chance to work things through, or as her friend Michelle said, just the more obvious transition toward acceptance of a divorce. Lucky nodded in agreement to attending the appointment, but when the day came, he was sitting in Abby's living room with a glass he kept refilling from the box of wine on the kitchen counter.

His behavior didn't bother Abby, the way it bothered Grace. She knew he was hurt, and that was something they had in common. Their times together could have been dominated by bitterness, but in actuality they were quite tender. They just seemed to fit, and to make sense.

Lucky, feeling that this new thing was important, started coming out of the helpless feelings he was having and feeling like a human being again. He felt he was nothing special, no longer with savant-type luck, but also without the despair of losing his luck. Life could be good with this woman.

Abby also, saw the potential of not being isolated and lonely. It was one of her biggest fears, that she would die alone—which was one of the reasons she decided to adopt Manny, so that she wouldn't feel alone. She still had her moments, mostly when Lucky left to go home to Grace, but Grace's displeasure of Lucky's dog, Bingo, now left her with two resentments. She viewed her relationship with Lucky as a commitment and was protective of him.

The last time Lucky went home, Grace told him about the next upcoming appointment. Lucky was embarrassed about missing the last one, as his intention was not to be passive aggressive or even just plain aggressive by missing it. He looked at Grace, who locked eyes with his, her body leaning away from him, as she held out the appointment card. Lucky took it, not totally unexpected, and read the business card of Attorney Bradley Grabowski, Divorce Attorney. The appointment was in two days, so Lucky, with that time scheduled, packed a bag and drove his BMW back to Abby's house.

Section 2, Part I

Candace

1

Shootings

In America, shootings, which were many and often, seemed like a punch in the gut for newly-minted Congresswoman Candace Malone. After all, her platform supported guns in the hands of everyone, because it was their right to carry any gun they could get their hands on. She was solid on this message, as she was a bright new star.

It seemed that all were in favor of her rally behind this. All except her. It made her miserable after researching the victims, in case a question was asked of her about any of them. Afterwards, she'd fall into the agony of knowing things might have been prevented. It depressed her. Gun advocates played the mental health card in all these killings, but Candace knew that even so, people weren't being, and couldn't be, screened by professionals before their purchase. Anyone could buy anything, and there was nothing that could be done. America was great.

Candace questioned the circular logic that formed around the mental health argument. Of course, no one sane would shoot up a church, school, mall, or nightclub. It was hard to conceive the mindset of a shooter. Were they depressed, getting back at the world in general, or were they psychotic, without knowing the reality of what they were doing even while planning to do it? Then, again, the issue of mental health rights. Are we to prevent anyone with a mental health diagnosis from living their lives without scrutiny or much worse? Candace knew that once you went to a therapist for any reason, they had to give you a diagnosis, or else they couldn't treat you—it really was the opposite of how it should be. Instead of treating a diagnosis with therapy, a person would get a diagnosis because they were trying to better themselves. And, which diagnosis would we need to remove someone from society or implant some sort of Anti-gun-buying chip into their forehead? Wouldn't that be against their rights? Also, this would end up being a system of self-reporting because of HIPAA regulations, a list of those with various diagnoses that would be accessible to any gun retail outlet.

Candace concluded that none of this could be effectively regulated. Decreasing the numbers of victims was a tried-and-true historical fact that came with gun restrictions. It was something to really look at. The argument gun advocates always used shifted to how *all* shootings were impossible to prevent, 100% of them, which was true. They never looked at any decrease in numbers: *You see, what good are your restrictions because people are still getting shot or knifed all the time.* Even their argument of mass-knifings, in which people would just use knives or cars if guns were taken away, was true and could be argued, but the big fact was always missed: the correlation of decreasing guns also decreased the total number of shooting victims. This always was true.

Candace's stomach hurt, and it felt like a prickly sweat was beading up on her scalp, much like when you sweat from eating spicy food. Not only was she still spewing out facts on the gun side of things, to promote her political career, she saw personal, positive results of that manipulation. She wanted to have a nap.

It was much easier to be all in on the other big issue, her Pro-Life stance. Her own or anyone else's aborted fetuses never were shown on Fox, and no one at CNN was asking for a comment from her. When there was a mass shooting, it got as much gruesome coverage as possible...until the next shooting occurred. It was good for ratings. Nevertheless, her talking points about this were keeping her politically relevant and giving her income. Not that her civil-service job was going to be all that lucrative, but the Pro-gun lobby money to continue to "speak the truth" was getting larger and larger in amount. Lobbyist, paid her almost weekly. One of them even bought her a new car.

After another review of victims and their lives, the "Just Win" her husband always spouted at her was starting to gnaw at her, churning in her brain as bad as *Just Win at Any Cost* or even worse, *Just Win, because anything you actually believe doesn't mean a fuck.* She had sold out. Every new shooting made her sick, but she couldn't quit being the hot, new, star spokeswoman for the NRA.

And then another shooting happened, one more terrible than usual, because it was one in which children were involved. A man who hadn't been able to get past high school went back to Sunrise Elementary School, his old school, and opened fire, killing six teachers and twenty-five students. Immediately, there was a call for thoughts and prayers, followed by a call for keeping those with mental health issues locked up before more tragedies occurred, even though no one knew the background of the shooter. Immediately, there was a call for teachers to carry guns to fight off attackers. Immediately, there was the gaslighting of the parents of the young so that their crusade against semi-automatic weapons and realistic mental health screenings could be deflected. Immediately, Fox News stopped covering the parents and the victims and what they had to say.

   Candace Malone immediately needed a sick day, but sick days couldn't happen after something like this. Again, she had to speak her talking points, but keep them brief. She found herself saying she planned to meet with some of the parents of the children from Sunrise Elementary School. Common sense would call for her to wait a bit, so that the parents could grieve, or even start the process, but it was that sick feeling in the pit of her stomach that caused Candace's need to meet them as soon as possible. She needed to ease the feeling of helplessness, that even in her position, she couldn't do anything for anyone. She knew she could, yet couldn't bring herself to do it.

2

Dreams

Two days before meeting with the parents, Candace had a dream that she was high in the sky and falling. She was falling at a great speed, but at some points in the dream she was flying horizontally, as if she had wings. The part of her mind that was attached to reality in her dream state reminded her that she couldn't fly; instead, she was back being propelled quickly to the Earth's surface. Then she knew what was next, just like anyone does who is having an anxiety-laced life and a falling dream. She pulled the cord of her parachute, but there was no parachute being deployed. The ground was coming up, quicker and quicker, and Candace kept pulling the cord, and then, there was a chute. The parachute sprung out from the backpack, straight and true above her like a missile. Candace tilted her head back to look up, as the parachute remained straight, and true...unopened. There must be time, she thought, so she looked back to the ground, and in a millisecond, she hit.

She woke in a panic and out of sorts. No one hits the ground in a dream. It's not supposed to happen. *Fucking-dammit-helpless-struggle. What can I really do about it? I know why I'm having this dream. There's nothing I can do right now.*

On the morning she met with the victims of Sunrise Elementary's parents Candace had another dream. She knew it was anxiety-based once again. This time she was in a classroom by herself. The cranked windows were almost flat at 90 degrees, but only hot summer air was evident in the room, without any breeze coming through the windows. She went down the hall to the water fountain, and in full gear was a shooter walking away from her. He wore some sort of religious t-shirt that she couldn't make out. She had a walkie-talkie and spoke into it, telling the person on the other end that she was going to do what the school trained her to do, and to charge him.

"It's what the training video told us to do," she said to him.

The person on the other end of the headset was Bobby-Joe telling her to stay in place, and to not do anything, but it was too late. She charged the shooter from behind, but her teacher shoes slipped on the polished hallway floor, leaving her with one high-heeled shoe on, and one off, lying on the ground directly behind the shooter. The shooter turned and laughed...took aim...and before he could fire, Candace had a thought that she didn't care one bit about whether she got shot or not, life itself was minimal. This is the thought that Candace Malone woke up to, and she had to change it.

3
Conflict

When she was first told of it, Candace imagined that she would be meeting privately with sets of parents, one pair at a time, and it would be at her office, intimate and private. What she didn't imagine was that it was set up in a Town Hall type of meeting, with each parent giving an emotional victim statement, which of course involved the television news, with cameras rolling. She did go into her office, but it was for Fox News debriefing her. Candace took a deep breath and prepared herself for seeing the stuffed animals, trophies, pictures of sons or daughters, being held and the tears of the parents. She coached herself in how to handle her own reaction to the parents' breaking down during their declarations. Yes, there was going to be plenty of that, but she wasn't prepared for the open anger, and the open outrage, directed to her and other legislators. Every single parent knew exactly where she publicly stood on the gun rights issue, and Candace had an overwhelming urge to run.

But, she couldn't. She was on live TV. Her constituents did their jobs staying within party lines, but Candace wanted nothing more than to be herself, to show empathy, and to offer help. Her politics stood on the opposite side of the parents who bravely spoke of their lost children while completely falling apart. And then there was a statement from a subdued mother, wearing a MAGA cap, and a matching TRUMP t-shirt, holding a set of clothes belonging to her daughter. She shifted uncomfortably and, in a low, quiet, difficult-to-hear voice began:

I stand before you today with a heavy heart, a grieving soul, and a voice that trembles with both sorrow and determination. My name is Juliet Debrusk, and I am the parent of Ophelia, whose beautiful life was tragically extinguished in the mass shooting that recently took place. I am here to share not only my personal grief but also the collective pain of countless families who have been irrevocably shattered by acts of senseless violence.

The loss of my child, my Ophelia, is a wound that will never heal. Ophelia was 10 years old, full of life, dreams, and a future that held infinite possibilities. But those possibilities were violently ripped away by an act of cruelty that defies all understanding. My Ophelia, like your own children, should have been allowed to grow, to learn, to love, and to make their mark on this world. Instead, many of you have worked against this and forever silenced this potential. We are left with anger, grief, and the haunting question of why this happened and what could have been done differently to prevent it.

I implore you to take meaningful action. We must come together, across party lines, to enact comprehensive gun safety measures that keep deadly weapons out of the hands of those who seek to harm innocent lives. I understand that the Second Amendment is an important aspect of our nation's history and values, but the lives of our children, the lives of our loved ones, are invaluable. We must invest in mental health resources, address the root causes of violence, and enhance background checks to prevent dangerous individuals from acquiring firearms.

I stand here today with Ophelia's clothes in my trembling hand, a constant reminder of how her life ended. I ask each of you to hold this image in your hearts as you deliberate and make decisions that will shape the future of our nation. I speak not just for myself but for the countless parents, siblings, friends, and loved ones who are united in grief and who long for a world where mass shootings can be a thing of the past.

Thank you.

As Juliet Debrusk said her thank-you, she unwrapped the clothes she was holding, which were removed from her daughter at the funeral home, the clothes she demanded not be washed. Juliet Debrusk burst into tears, burying her face into the bloody, stained clothes of her daughter, the wailing too loud, too uncomfortable on the television microphone, yet still heard after the mic was cut. Most of the television news outlets cut away at this point, but Juliet's tears had soaked into her daughter's dried blood. When she lifted her face away there was a faint smear of red on Juliet's face. It was an unintentional act, causing a memorable image that ended up on the front page of national newspapers and the lead story of all media outlets. Her blood-painted face would be a photo frozen in historic time. Then there were some words, no longer subdued, which launched out of her, "The blood is on me. The blood is on you!" It was an unintentional act that was much more influential than the words of her prepared speech.

Then there was another act, this one unintentional, that caused a stir in the news. There was another frozen image, this one showing Candace Malone, Pro-gun advocate, crying with one hand covering her mouth.

4

How To Resolve Conflict

The right-leaning newspapers which had Candace's picture, complete with running eyes and disordered hair, posted under headlines such as *BLEEDING HEART*, while the more liberal outlets promoted their periodicals with *CHANGE OF HEART*. Candace didn't want to read about herself in either which way, although she felt drawn more to *CHANGE OF HEART* than *BLEEDING HEART*. She also hated how she looked in the photos, weak, unkempt, and not dignified. These thoughts held her to pause, as why out of all the undignified things politicians were recently up to, crying with her usually neat, long, brown hair pulled up in a messy bun seemed bad to her. She had based her entire successful political career on strength, appearance, the physical, even more than how she represented issues. She knew she needed to move to a place of strength, and that place was to be *in* her office, and *with* Juliet Debrusk in a 1:1 situation.

But Juliet was hard to nail down. She was appearing on news shows and talk shows everywhere one might look. When she wasn't busy advocating for gun regulations, she was hiding from aggressive gun supporters yelling about their rights, politicians who needed to appease their supporters, and hardcore religious groups, such as the group *Guns for Nuns*, who now had strong political power as a voter base. The *Guns for Nuns* group was mostly extreme right-wing Christians who used their religious base for political gain. Most of the t-shirt-wearing group would seem to be more comfortable in sleeveless cut flannel shirts and hunting gear, though many of them never hunted. More surprising were the women aged thirty and over who supported *Guns for Nuns*, but looked more likely to appear in the pages of *Woman's Day Magazine* than firing off clips of ammunition. But there they were, pictured in their social-media profiles, holding semi-automatic weapons, sometimes posing with their children, also supporting their Second Amendment rights.

Candace's staff began to research Juliet Debrusk. What they uncovered was that even though Sunrise Elementary School was hundreds of miles away, before moving, Juliet and Ophelia had incredibly lived in Candace's district. *I wonder if she knew this?* Candace thought. *It must be some sort of destiny.*

The staff also were forced to reach Juliet Debrusk through her publicist, who didn't understand that a personal meeting with Candace Malone was not a paid appearance. "Maybe when we need another bump, when things die down a bit, she can meet with Congresswoman Malone," was the follow-up response. When her aides delivered that message, Candace felt an uncomfortable tingle when the words "die down" were uttered.

Candace decided to do what politicians do, which was to wade through the muck and get Juliet's direct email, the one she used when she first reached out to appear at the Town Hall Meeting. She began to type:

Dearest Juliet

She then moused-over that and hit delete.

Dear Ms. Debrusk

Although we've never met, you've probably seen the pictures of me being deeply moved by your speech at the Town Hall. What you probably don't know is that you used to live in my district, which means that there are people still here that may know you. These are my people, so I consider you that as well. I want you to know that I heard you, and your message. I would like to invite you to meet with me privately to discuss this issue and what we can do to prevent further accidents from occurring. I could never understand what you are going through, but I'd like to be your ally, and I hope you respond with any available times you have to meet.

Blessings,
Candace Malone

Candace moused over the word *Blessings*, hit delete, typed *With Deepest Sympathy*, only to delete that as well. She decided on the word *Sincerely* and hit send.

Juliet responded immediately.

Mrs. Malone,

How dare you use the word accident while at the same time inviting me to discuss this "issue". This was NOT an accident, and the loss of my daughter was NOT an issue, it was a preventable murder. I am available early next week, specifically Tuesday at 11 AM, to come to Washington and speak with you. I believe this conversation is necessary, and I will be very direct with what I will say to you. I do not wish this to be a photo opportunity for you, with us both sipping tea and nibbling delightfully on fancy snacks.

God Bless,
Juliet Debrusk

Candace was caught off guard by the quickness of her response or at being rebuked. Certainly, Juliet had to see that this wasn't intended to promote the GOP agenda, and to influence her in any way. Candace *did* expect her to be the same bulldog as she was in some of her television appearances, and a champion for gun control. Juliet needed to know directly from her that Candace Malone was there to support her and give her an ear, even a shoulder to rest upon. Candace was readying herself to hear her privately so that Juliet could have hope for the future. Candace Malone knew that this very sentiment would, as much as she wanted it to, not make her feel very clean; in fact, it was a total pool of shit.

5

How People Can Change

On the day of her meeting with Juliet, Candace decided to dress casual: A t-shirt, jeans, with her hair hanging down, not clipped or styled in any way. When she entered her office, just ten minutes before Juliet Debrusk was to be escorted in, she saw what was laid out by her staff. The office had two very fancy Windsor Court arm chairs. Between the two chairs was a very fancy service for tea, adorned with rose patterns on the thin-lipped dainty cups. To top it off there was a tri-pod set up directly in front of them, about twenty feet away.

Candace's mouth hung open, and for a few seconds she was unable to speak, but when she did, the words, "Get this all the fuck out of here! Right now!" flew out of her mouth unexpectedly, like a dragon expelling fire. The staff flew in and removed the tea service and the camera setup. A saucer bounced off the carpet without breaking. Candace wanted the chairs left where they were, but facing each other instead of tilting at the thirty-degree angles of the original placement. She liked the chairs. She certainly didn't want to give off the impression of power over her guest by sitting across from Juliet, behind her large mahogany desk with a large gold nameplate complete with her title in front of her.

Candace sat down and took a deep breath. She then realized that her fingers had been picking at a narrow skintag on her right temple. When she pulled her hand back, she noticed a faint trail of blood on her pointer finger. She got up and raced for a Kleenex and pressed it against the pinpoint. Glancing at herself in the mirror, she realized her outfit looked like one Jimmy Carter might wear while building houses for Habitat for Humanity. *Too late to do anything about that now*, she thought as she hustled back to her desk and barked into the intercom. "Don't send Ms. Debrusk in if she's here already!" But it was too late as Sally, in her tight blue business suit, was already showing Juliet Debrusk into the office.

"I'm sorry," Sally, standing extremely erect, answered. "Do you want me to...?"

"No, it's OK," Candace said, more cooly than she intended. Her urgent expression melted into a smile as she pulled the tissue off the cut and greeted Juliet, inviting her to sit down. "I'm sorry, I have a small cut and was hoping to have time to stop the bleeding."

Juliet Dubrusk was silent, and remained so as Candace positioned herself in the chair next to hers. "Remember when we were kids and the only trouble we could get into was passing notes, chewing gum, or spitballs?" Juliet glared at her, the icebreaking attempt by Candace a complete failure.

"You called me here," Juliet said, breaking the awkward silence. "I don't think you can compare any of this to—"

Candace interrupted her, "Yes. What can I do to

help?"

"You can get on the right side of this...I mean, correct side."

"I think I am. I just can't be out there. I'd lose my seat, then I wouldn't be able to help anyone," Candace explained.

Juliet's mouth became terse. "I really don't give a shit about you being here or not being here. All I care about is that something is done to remove, or, make more difficult, the owning of assault rifles. They are just there to kill, not to arm any invisible militia."

"I know—" Candace began.

"It's bullshit!" Juliet yelled out suddenly, the sound echoing through Candace's office, then dissolving into weighted silence, the excruciating pause lasting ten seconds, the time it took for Juliet's anger to decelerate temporarily. "I know how you were moved by my comments at Town Hall. In fact, the entire country saw it. You can't backpedal now! You want to do something, then stand up for what you believe in! My daughter is dead! It's too late for her!"

Candace remained silent, pushing her spine against the back of her chair. She felt frozen, and powerless. Then she realized it had again been quiet when she heard Juliet weeping. Candace started to hand her the tissue she had pressed against her bloody temple, but then saw the spots of on it, and got up to retrieve some fresh tissues. She knew Juliet was right. She handed Juliet a wad of tissues she had yanked out of the box and began to talk.

6
The Reveal

When the red-eyed Juliet left the Cannon House Office Building, her puffy eyes and despair had been noticed. Though her meeting with Candace Malone hadn't been public knowledge, both CNN and Fox News accidently caught her leaving her meeting with Rep Malone and rushed in with their microphones.

Juliet managed a smile. "I have a new and somewhat surprising ally, Representative Candace Malone."

"What did she say?" asked the CNN reporter.

"Representative Malone assured me that she will fight for stricter gun regulation, up to and including the banning of assault rifles for public use."

The Fox reporter leapt in. "Is she now disapproving of the Constitution's Second Amendment?"

"She's just going to help, Juliet said, as she noticed the Fox reporter about to jump in with another loaded question. "And fuck your ratings-grubbing agenda, throwing a question like that in there."

Walking away she overheard, *Well, we apologize for the use of profanity, but the mother of slain student Ophelia*

Debrusk has told us that Representative Candace Malone has jumped to the side of all true Americans...." Juliet Debrusk walked faster, to be far enough away not to have to hear any more of his unrelated diatribe.

※ ※ ※

Candace's cell phone was ringing. She sent it to voice mail and then it immediately rang again. She was not ready to make an official statement. Not today. When she went to see who was calling, the name HUSBAND appeared on the home screen. She may not have been ready to make an official statement to the world, but she was ready to do so to her husband, no matter how mad he got. Instead, when she answered, his voice was calm.

"It's OK, Honey. We'll work with this."

"You aren't mad are you?" and then she finally process what he had just said, "Huh?" she stammered.

"It's done. We can work with this. We have to," Bobby-Joe said.

"I don't necessarily care if there is a spin. I just want to be honest," Candace said.

"We will amp up the rest of what our voters want, and concentrate on the victims...concentrate on the number of shootings...concentrate on how un-American it is to have innocent Americans shot and killed. We still will support the forming of militias, and The Second Amendment, but not support the ability of people to randomly kill people," he said. You will then say, "Also, my dear friend Juliet Debrusk, formerly from my district, has given me the courage to get behind, *Ophelia's Bill*, which will...,"

"Hold on. Hold on. Hold on. It sounds like you are making my statement for me," Candace said.

"Are you writing this down?"

"Bobby-Joe, I think I can come up with something

like this on my own, if I'm just being honest, and I intend on just being honest from now on." She'd much rather have said her original instinct, *"Goddamn it, stop being condescending!"*

He picked up on it. "OK, Honey, I'm just trying to...."

"Wait, wait," Candace cut in, "I can use 'my friend formerly from my district'...and *Ophelia's Bill*? Can we do an *Ophelia's Bill*?"

Suddenly, a call came in from a number that she thought was Juliet Debrusk's. Candace took a breath, instantly rehearsing what she might say to her. Where exactly was the line in her public stance being drawn, and what about this fresh new idea about *Ophelia's Bill*? What would it do exactly? Could she tell her? She needed more time on that one, as Juliet would spill everything to the media everything she was about to tell her. Candace knew that.

"Hold on, Bobby-Joe," I have to take this. When Candace picked up the call, there was not a calm voice on the other side.

"FUCK YOU, CUNT!!!," the man's voice from the other side screamed at her and hung up.

7

Tightrope

Bobby-Joe thought it was just a news outlet looking to talk to her, but Candace stood there with a blank face after hanging up without speaking.

"It was a man," she finally said.

"What outlet was he from?" Bobby-Joe asked.

"It was an angry white man calling me the 'C' word," Candace mumbled.

"Well, you know you're going to face some backlash."

"He called me the 'C' word," Candace repeated flatly. Inside she was seething.

"Do we need to develop a strategy?" Bobby-Joe asked.

"No," she said. "*We* don't. I do, but we fucking don't."

Then Bobby-Joe did exactly what she wanted. He said, "I'm behind you. Let me know if there's anything I can do to support you."

※ ※ ※

Even without an official statement from Candace, the headlines and television media screamed about her meeting with Juliet Debrusk. Public opinion was mixed, and as opinionated as expected, but the most damning of rhetoric was by the mid to extreme, Conservative, right-wing channels who vilified her as one of the biggest traitors in the history of the United States. Candace Malone was painted as Anti-American, Anti-constitution, and the enemy to all the God-loving, flag-waving, America is Great Again patriots. Most in Congress agreed with her, and a quick poll also concluded that she was on the correct side of this. *And the rest can fuck themselves*, Candace thought.

She knew she had to make a statement while this was still hot and before something else would grab the headlines. Of course, that could easily be another shooting, but she hoped for that not to happen. Candace had to make a statement that would minimize the damage from both sides of the argument. To her, the end game of both sides supporting her point of view was one that would be impossible to achieve, but if played correctly would appeal the general vote of both sides.

Damage control in this situation would be found in talking about restrictions of high-powered artillery while speaking highly of Americans defending themselves. It would also be found on the other side of keeping guns away from crazy people, people not like you and me, but those who are so off-centered they would mow down the good Americans and their children. There were better ways to protect ourselves Proactively than to defend ourselves with opposite fire power. Candace began to write her statement, but as she sat there, the image of Juliet Debrusk holding the bloody clothes to her face caused her to revise her point of view. *I can't do this, I can't do this*, she thought while playing with the metal American flag pin mounted like a trophy on the collar of her blouse. Candace deleted what she had written and created a manifesto that Juliet Debrusk and all the other parents would be proud of. She ended her statement with, "Catch you on the flip side," as a playful nod to her changing her point of view. She loaded her statement into the massive media and news email list, and hit Send. She breathed a sigh of relief and said out loud to an empty room, "It is finished." Candace felt at peace and was not in fear of any backlash or being crucified in the media. She anticipated it. She got up, poured herself a glass of wine, but didn't drink it. She more wanted something to quench her thirst, so she poured the wine down the sink and opened the refrigerator.

8
Answering A Phone Call

Even though the name that came up on her cell phone display read, "MOM" Candace was still worried that it might be a trick. Maybe the caller was using a cell phone number scrambling system that would bring up displayed names on phones, even if they were from different number. Candace pretty much had stopped answering her phone altogether, but this time she picked up.

After the dueling hellos, her mother jumped in, "You know, you probably should have handled that with more clandestineness than you did."

"So, you're calling me to be critical?" Candace questioned.

"Let's just say there is some damage that should have been controlled, and God knows the Taylors have already controlled enough of that," Mary Taylor said.

"Yes, Mom, I know the history of that. I was a part of it."

"Yes, Candace, we don't need to bring that up."

"You're the one that brought it—"

"All I'm saying, is now people will take a deeper dive. I've already seen on the internet the fear you're changing your Pro-Life stance, and then it's only a matter of time that things get unturned. I hear the Democrats hire investigators to go through all of the records of people that they can," her mother warned her.

"Ohhhh, *the internet*," Candace jumped in sarcastically. "You must believe what you read on the internet. You know, I try to stay away from it."

"It's true. They have all kinds of bots and things that can instantly find your past."

"Mother. I believe that there is no record of my abortion. Remember you didn't use my name?' Candace replied, perturbed.

"But there may be pictures and factual recognition taken from some Google satellite or something," Mary said.

"Mom."

"What about drones?"

"Jesus, Mom, relax. I've got this under control, and look...besides believing what you read on the internet, you should probably stop watching TV as well."

"I watch the news. How else can I keep up with all the terrible things they are saying about my daughter," Mary said.

"Mom, goodbye," Candace said and hung up, while thinking if it only could be that easy to handle the other more aggressive people who might be calling her on her cell phone.

9

Freefall

If the telephone call, in which she was called 'the C word' was the worst thing that was going to happen, Candace Malone would be lucky. Officially, she had changed sides on one of the most polarizing issues in the country. When Bobby-Joe posted for her on social media, she read the posts but never read any of the responses. They were all too brutal. When Candace wanted to feel better, she would read Tweets from the parents, relatives, and friends of gun victims. She also would read the Tweets and responses of those who were at shooting locations and survived. Candace gathered strength from those who have been through far worse than bullying on the internet. Even the hard-liner Christian group *Guns for Nuns* was openly hostile against any posts to her account.

If this all ruins my career, she thought. *I'm sure there are some news talk shows I can always become a part of.*

Her new supporters had commented how brave she was. *That's nice but that won't get me past even one round of the next election.* Still, it was pretty nice of the new followers to speak up, even if her approval numbers amongst her core voters were dropping like a stone released from the roof of a tall building. *I'm still one of you*, she wanted to argue in the comments, but in reality, she knew she wasn't. She also knew she was not the weak Republican or Anti-American she was being accused of. She still wore the flag pin on her lapel, no matter how loud the yelling was about it. She would never back down.

"Let's go out to eat. We should celebrate," Bobby-Joe said.

"I don't think that's such a good idea," Candace replied.

"People need to see you out there and not hiding. Come on, I made reservations at Decisione Deliziosa."

Candace was nervous. Even though she wasn't officially hiding, she had not tried to go about her day-to-day business openly. *Maybe,* she thought. *Maybe everything will be OK with Bobby-Joe there. After all, he made some of the strongest Pro-gun statements in my campaign, so this might be a good buffer.*

✻ ✻ ✻

Slowly Candace regained the confidence to live her life and to appear to be living it as normally as possible. Yes, there were more angry phone calls, so she had to change her cell phone number multiple times, each time after her private number went public. Yes, there were the same type of messages left at her office on the work line, but her aides never filled her in to the amount of, and the intensity of, the horrible vitriol. Her aids had a wide-open contact with the FBI regarding some of the more expressive threats.

When she did go out in public the trolls would post a picture and her location on social media. Bobby-Joe told her not to read the comments underneath each posting but all Candace had to do was see that over 14,000 commented and 3-4,000 shared the post. Bobby-Joe, on the other hand, read each and every comment. He didn't respond to them, but he would post new statements for Candace, re-iterating her position and support for responsible gun ownership and the right to bear arms. His posts were often met with memes suggesting Candace being a traitor or a Communist. The memes also suggested incorrectly that she had changed her views on other things, such as health care 'LYNCH THE SOCIALIST!' and Pro-Life 'TWO-FACE MALONE' and 'BABY KILLER MALONE' often used as a not so clever play on Baby Face Malone).

"It's just people expressing their frustration," Bobby-Joe told her over their light afternoon meal and a few glasses of wine. Bobby-Joe's phone was blowing up, as it did anytime they were out in public. "Coming soon: Pictures of us having lunch," he said to her, but she didn't even smile. "Well, we can rally around this and First Amendment Rights, if you so choose."

"If we have to. Seems that the more I, and actually you, post, the more aggressive the underlying hate becomes. I think the strategy is to slip undercover for a little and see if it blows over. My numbers are going down right now."

"I dunno, that might be temporary. With the numbers of shootings these days, you can be a voice which can satisfy everyone. It can be groundbreaking! Most people like you. You should see the comments about me. *"Her husband is not good enough"* And, I had to shut off the direct message feature because you were getting dick pics."

"I was getting WHAT???" Candace exclaimed.

"Well, a powerful woman, thin, and with looks like yours—"

"—gets dick pics? What the hell!"

"Well, yeah. Hate to keep that important stuff away from you while you serve the people, but you've been getting them for a long time. I mean, men are horrible. Look, for example, at the demographics of the typical mass-shooter...they are the same demographic that sends dick pics. Anyway, don't feel bad. I'm the one that should feel bad. I hardly measure up to most of them."

Candace didn't know what to say to any of that. She didn't want to say anything to him, almost as if he were the one sending the pictures instead of the one seeing them and not telling her about them. *That's not a compliment. IF Bobby-Joe feels that is some sort of backwards compliment then he is almost as bad.*

The table was silent. Candace became very aware of the sounds of forks on plates, and the ice in the drinking glasses tinkled. She was also aware of some movement near the hostess's section and a beefy woman, with a well-worn fatigue cap, faded out red t-shirt and vest who strode quickly right toward their table. The shirt read, *Guns for Nuns,* with a nun wearing a habit and holding a rifle. It was almost hard to process as Candace sat frozen, cappuccino at half-mast with an initial thought, not of fear, being, *This person is not dressed for this type of establishment.* That thought was followed up with *I hope nothing happens to Bobby-Joe*, as her husband stood up to position himself between the woman and Candace. The woman never got that close though. It wasn't because she was stopped by anyone; it was because she stopped to shout something at Candace from fifteen feet away, which was so loud and distorted that it was incomprehensible. Her yelling also wasn't stopped by anyone, because the people in the busy restaurant all sat there taking pictures and video to post on social media.

10

The Final Statement of Belief in Nicene

It wasn't much of a stretch to say Candace Malone was worried. Worried, but not scared. The only real fear she had was going to sleep. Her nightmares had become, as she would like to say, an inconvenience and a burden. Often, when she dozed off, she would end up springing up out of bed, her thick and neat public display of hair now sticking and stringy on her forehead. Sometimes she would also be yelling, crying, or screaming, without remembering the nightmare's content and why those responses were being elicited. And then in the morning the symptoms didn't seem to stop. Eating breakfast, it seemed that she couldn't stop sweating. She hadn't done anything except spoon some cereal into her mouth and drink coffee, but her ability to thermoregulate seemed to be broken. She was grateful for Bobby-Joe, who remained her rock through all this. He was the one holding her, calming her in the middle of the night. He was the one there to reassure her that this was a temporary bump and all things were going to be alright. If he was worried about any of what was going on, he didn't let on. Candace thought she might have quit politics, or not have moved on in her career, if it hadn't been for Bobby-Joe's belief in her and keeping her focused on the prize. Bobby-Joe pushed her to remain in the public eye, to be relevant and not shrink away with her beliefs.

Candace would leave each morning, making sure she was beyond looking *put-together*. Her suits were well-tailored, forming tight lines to her tall, powerful, strong and attractive frame. Her make-up wasn't overstated or understated but professional and style. If she weren't the center of such a controversy, she would be turning heads for her looks alone.

She also was encouraged to be approachable. People wanted autographs, mostly now liberals, and she was a bit embarrassed by their requests. She felt uncom-fortable stopping, because then she may have to answer off-the-cuff questions, but on the other hand, she didn't want to brush people off who were just wanting to feel important or to take home a trophy. The haters that wanted to yell at her when she exited from her vehicle usually did so across the street. They weren't looking for her to stop, only wanting to disturb her. She was fine with that, and also fine with protesters. Bobby-Joe said they weren't protesting her, per se, but rather aggres-sively chanting out their own beliefs. The most aggres-sive were the *Guns for Nun-ers,* who were energized by broadcast media to fight for America and American values. They always seemed to be wherever she was, either in large groups or individually, and they all dressed and acted the same, hard to even tell they were unique individuals anymore. They were very noisy, mob-like, and decidedly not, as Candace viewed them, very Christian. Increasingly, as she remained out in public, and received loads of coverage around every move, com-plete with negative tele-prompts at the bottom of screen, the protests became louder and angrier. She had never even heard of *Guns for Nuns* until she became their traitor, and that group member stormed into the restaurant she and Bobby-Joe hoped to have a sense of normalcy at. *I don't know what God they believed in, but it certainly isn't a God that loving Christians would believe in. It certainly wasn't a God my parents prayed to,* she thought.

Which brought her to The Summit Church in Springfield, Virginia. Pastor Timothy Edgars had contacted her to bring a message to the parishioners of love and hope.

"This is the perfect opportunity to talk about not killing church-going Americans with semi-automatic weapons. You can talk about the right to bear arms, for *good* people and the Constitution," Bobby-Joe said on their way to the church. "It even begins, We the People of the United States, in Order to form a more perfect Union, establish Justice, ensure domestic Tranquility, provide for the common defense, promote the general Welfare, and secure the Blessings of Liberty to ourselves and our Posterity, do ordain and establish this Constitution for the United States of America."

"I know what it says," she said flatly, smoothing the front of her better than well put-together suit.

"I mean, justice, tranquility, and blessing!" he trumpeted.

"I know the talking parts," she said, but really wanted to tell him how sick of him she was becoming.

Candace hurried out of the limo, and Bobby-Joe almost reached out to pull her back in, to get a handle of the conversation, but he was too late; she had stepped out and she was exposed. During her quibbling with Bobby-Joe, she hadn't noticed the person standing a few parking spaces away, a man with the red *Guns for Nuns* t-shirt and a well-worn, fatigue patterned hat. Candace Malone was out in the fresh air and now saw him, about ten yards away, hunched over. At first Candace thought it was the same woman from the restaurant, but the masculine familiarity around him, when he suddenly stood erect, made the hair stand up on the back of her neck. *Have I ever seen him before? I know I know you.* Candace told herself, but she couldn't identify him, because he had a black wind-guard over his face. She suddenly felt the way one does when they forget what to say in a conversation, and the thought never comes back to you. She felt naked with him standing there, suddenly tall, upright. *This is not at all like the woman at the restaurant, taller—stronger—and....*

And she suddenly knew. The gun, not being a semi-automatic, was the last thought she had before her body suddenly started shuddering. She didn't have a chance to hear the number of shots which rang out. She heard a quick pop, and briefly felt the tinge of the first of many rounds entering her, and then the split-second realization on why her body had moved involuntarily. She saw flashes of light—body dancing, then soaring, and soaring, and soaring above her, while she viewed her own dead body on her way to the afterlife.

Section 1, Part II

Peter

1
The Blame Game

Peter was home, and he wasn't going to get caught. What he had worn was so generic that the only thing tying him to his act was a red t-shirt, but so many of those had been sold, and the group had become so large, it was almost non-identifying.

A few days ago, when his window crashed onto him, someone had to be at fault. Felton was at fault, but he certainly couldn't go after him. The next day he had an appointment with his therapist. After shutting himself down, Peter was so agitated he was able to go off with his anger about Nick Felton. Kelly Granta told him that going after his neighbor would be a huge mistake. Peter was enraged when she told him that, as his statement was more about what he wanted to do than a recognition of a flaw within him that he had to work on. Peter had completely given up on working on flaws. He also agreed that it was a bad idea to go after Nick Felton, that nothing good could come out of it. Someone had to be blamed, because someone was at fault. Could it be the house? Was the house at fault? That seemed crazy to him, until he made a jump to why he was even at this point in the first place. Peter understood the connection. Why he ended up in that house, and the torture it had caused. He didn't mention any of that to Kelly Granta, only talking about Nick Felton. And yes it was a bad idea to crush Felton's neck in his bare hands, the cracking of the esophagus feeling like snapping a piece of plastic piping. Peter gestured in the office, his hands forming like brackets in the air for emphasis.

Kelly Granta agreed.

Yes, it was a bad idea to knock Felton down in his own kitchen, taking his heavy boot, striking down on Felton's head, which is what Peter stood and displayed in Kelly Granta's office, stomping down hard on unforgiving industrial carpet.

Kelly Granta agreed.

And, yes, yes, yes, it was a bad idea to break into Nick Felton's home by smashing his window and to pick up a shard of glass to stab him in the throat. It was a bad idea because if he got caught, and he would, he would be facing a long term in a maximum-security jail.

Kelly Granta agreed.

Kelly Granta saw this as progress in Peter. Being able to express oneself and realizing that is wrong to do, what he was expressing almost seemed more than progress. It was a breakthrough. It seemed like a normal way to discuss his anger via therapy. When she counseled couples struggling with their infidelity, she would gently talk about forgiving and how it is OK to have urges, even lustful thoughts, but not act out upon them. Even talking about these could be bad if the situation was not discussed as being a safe thing to discuss. Kelly Granta, as Peter was exploding and letting it out, had an overwhelming feeling that she was very good at her job.

What Peter didn't say to her was it was a bad idea to shoot Candace Malone, but he reasoned, the time for that was limited with politicians flip-flopping their views. Candace Malone, who had taken so much away from him, had the nerve to try to take one more thing, and it was all her fault.

Kelly Granta didn't agree with that, only because she had no idea. Kelly Granta believed she had created a change in Peter, and she was a success, because Peter, being a forensic assignment, was a case classified in her office as a tough cookie.

There were two classifications of cases in Kelly Granta's agency, which the staff liked to joke about. Either the case was easy, called a cupcake, or in cases assigned to them like Peter's, the tough cookies. Kelly Granta thought that by using dessert items to describe their caseload, it helped to lessen the stress and burnout of their jobs. Things could go either way in cases like Peter's, and at this moment, Kelly Granta felt the needle was moving quickly in the right direction, and it would only be a matter of time before he would be able to discuss Candace Malone's death, which was all over the news. It seemed funny to her that he had not mentioned it, mostly focusing on Nick Felton, but Kelly Granta felt that he would bring it up very soon, in the next few sessions. She knew that many of his reactions stemmed from the underlying difficulty of loving and hating a person at the same time. Since Candace, in Kelly Granta's opinion, was the defining moment of Peter's troubled life, she would not bring it up for him. He must do it.

Time here was also limited, as Peter had almost fulfilled the courts obligation, like the clock in her office that was as loud as a bomb. *Tick-Tick-Tick.*

2

Tick Tick Tick

Was Candace Malone's death preventable? Maybe Kelly Granta thought things were ticking in the right direction, but this was lost on Peter as he sat on his bed, staring at the boarded-up window. There were plenty of shifts in his therapy that led to it. Satisfying the requirement of counseling was almost over, and Peter had experienced many shifts in perspective. The first shift in his therapy process, the shift of him having a real shot for improvement, had shifted as quickly as it was realized when Kelly Granta's eyelids closed. It made him feel beyond help, but he still stuck to attending to just meet his court ordered requirement, which was the second shift. Basically, checking off the box was now replaced, in the back seat to his constant thoughts of Candace Taylor and Candace Malone, which talking to Kelly Granta seemed to produce after he was in her office, and they hadn't been talking about her. Not talking about her produced constant thoughts of her...which were full of guilty, shame, and remorse. Candace Taylor and Candace Malone now seemed like two different people to him. The part that was Candace Taylor seemed good, and the part that was Candace Malone seemed bad. Get rid of the bad and keep the good was a strategy Peter used, but what good was now left when the bad had been eliminated?

Her death was justifiable: Malone was the one that had moved on and started a successful new life without him. That was *bad*. And her husband? He was nothing at all like him, and for that matter, when exactly had they met? It was college. Vanderbilt. Peter knew because he researched it. It was when she put him in her rear-view mirror. It was the point Taylor ended and Malone began. It was the point that Peter's life was irreversibly ruined. It was also around that time when she changed her hair. Her look. She would not have looked like that if she had married him. Then there was her change in political views. This somehow represented everything bad about Candace Malone.

Therapy was supposed to be for his anger and impulse control. This was the goal of the court. Therapy, though, had done nothing to help with any of that. Kelly Granta thought that being able to talk about his anger would cause a breakthrough that would help him manage it. This was why the needle, to her, was moving in that direction. She didn't share that thought with Peter, and Peter wasn't really working on that as being the means to the end. He didn't have any goals anymore for therapy. You can't work on something if you don't know the how, what, where, and why of that arrangement. In fact, when he was home, he was worse than ever before. Kelly Granta couldn't see it. She thought the opposite, but Peter was angry enough to kill Nick Felton as well. Kelly Granta only saw progress, but she had no idea what she couldn't see and no idea how this "progress" was about to manifest. There were only two sessions left.

3
Hide and Seek

And it had manifested once already, which had caused Peter to develop a plan quickly. The drive from Nashville to The Great Smoky Mountains would take almost four hours. It would start at Nashville, bypass Cookville and Crossville, and head straight through Knoxville. Then it was a short jaunt south to reach the Smokies. This travel was all part of the plan, and Peter, when not acting out of anger and impulsivity, was a really good planner.

When he reached the Smoky Mountains, Peter planned to hike in and then bury the gun he used to kill Candace Malone. The red *Guns For Nuns* t-shirt, the jeans, the black face shield, and his fatigue cap were originally planned to be incinerated, but after various news outlets said how common his clothing worn was to that group, he concluded he was unidentifiable. He figured, based on his research, that only the gun, if it were to be found, would be uncovered accidentally years from now, long enough for him to be no longer be living. He had wiped it clean of any fingerprints, just in case, since, according to the news, a shooter had not been identified. Even if the gun was found tomorrow, it would be hard to link it to anyone. There were no suspects.

Peter also remembered everything of the shooting. It had all been planned. He was not in any blackout state, like he was in Nick Felton's house. It was a deliberate act he had known he was going to commit the second he started to think about Candace Malone because of Kelly Granta.

Days went by. There was still no new evidence, no surveillance video, and nothing that linked him to the assassination of Candace Malone. It was getting a lot of coverage, but according to eyewitnesses, he wasn't even described accurately. What the news said that authorities would be looking for was a man in either full fatigues or wearing a red bulletproof vest. The manhunt was also defined by looking for an African American. Peter knew the shirt was common, but the witnesses were even more off. He felt safe. There was no need for him to get rid of any of his clothing. All he had to do was not do anything that might cause any suspicion. He then heard something that made his skin crawl. Two voices he hadn't heard in a long time were on the news, and as Peter walked to the television, he saw Matthew and Mary Taylor in tears talking about how their lives had been changed forever. *Their lives? Their lives?* his head screamed at him. He then folded the clothes, the nuns on the t-shirt facing up, and waited for the Taylors to say the next insulting thing.

4
Discharge Meeting

Kelly Granta walked in, her turquoise and blue balloon pants with untied string ties jaunting around, below the waistband, like two ultra-thin people dancing. "You have fulfilled your requirement, attending the number of appointments the court has ordered, and we can discontinue therapy," she told him, as she sat, pushing her hairclip firmly against the back of her head until it began to hurt.

"So, I'm all set?" Peter Botchovich smirked. "I must be cured."

"Well," she said, using a winning smile when it was time for her to win either something or someone. "I will note the progress that you made, and I will conclude, to the court, that I feel you are not a problem to society." Kelly Granta slapped a sealed envelope, held in her right hand, into the palm of her left.

"Isn't that a danger to society?" he said, pushing his stringy hair out of his eyes, because he didn't want to look like a danger to society, even though he, unsuspected to her, was.

"Well, stating you as not being a problem would deduce that," Kelly Granta said, as she edged back in her leather desk chair, bothered that he had put her on the defensive.

"Alright," he grinned, which Kelly Granta concluded was him being proud of himself. So, she laid it on, "I think you've reached acceptance about much of your situation. I've written that to the court, and also, you are open to handling situations different ways.

"Thank you," he said, knowing he had pulled more than some wool, but an entire sheep over her eyes. It was something she deserved, being that she was part of the problem.

"I do want to mention, before we conclude, about something that has happened that you've not spoken about." Kelly Granta added.

"OK."

"Candace Malone. She was killed and you've chosen not to talk about it."

"She's dead to me," Peter said.

Kelly Granta wasn't sure if she was to take that literally or not, but, since her time with Peter was ending, added, "She's kind of dead to everyone," immediately wishing she hadn't said it. Her glib yet robotic response stopped his long-fingered grooming of his messy hair, and he felt himself getting angry at her matter-of-fact statement. Peter felt dismissed, waved away, but it was less the dismissiveness of him but than the dismissiveness of the fine work he had done in killing Candace Malone and not being caught. Although he couldn't tell her what the truth was, the feeling of the lack of importance of his act angered him.

"What the hell do you mean by that?" he said.

Kelly Granta's distinguished cheek bones pulsed as

if she were chewing gum. "Oh, I'm sorry I said that. Sure, cam we talk about Candace?"

"Maybe I don't want to talk about Candace. Maybe I don't want to talk about her being dead, or her being alive, or her fucking parents being on TV," Peter barked.

"I know you identify this as a loss."

"No. I don't."

Kelly Granta paused, and let the pause go ten seconds, fifteen...twenty...it seemed like forever. She felt like pushing him, something she had been reluctant to do, but since everything was winding down, she had nothing to lose.

"I think you do," she stated.

"No, I don't."

"Think about it. I think you do," Kelly Granta repeated five times until she noticed Peter's face becoming red.

"Do what? You think I do what?" his voice elevated.

What Kelly Granta never believed was that Peter would blackout when highly anxious or angry. She didn't even conclude it now, after Peter had crossed over and was only physically there with her. Peter's face now completely the color of a pomegranate as he stood, "You remind me of her!" he yelled.

Kelly Granta was not the type to look at things through one filter, so she tried to backpedal. Maybe Peter meant this in a good way. Candace Malone was a strong woman who was able to shift her beliefs. She was successful and attractive. She had power. She had enough power that someone was so much driven by it they wanted to kill her. And, they did. It was only then Kelly Granta realized she could be in danger. It wasn't the yelling, or the facial discoloration, but rather the connection she was making between Peter Botchovich and Candace Malone. The conclusion she made was like a flame touching gasoline. She needed to go to authorities regarding this, but that was just a thought at this point. "Did you kill her?"

She attempted to say it with a strong, firm voice, but instead, it came out angry and accusatory, so that the already agitated Peter moved toward the front edge of her desk. She had made a major error in judgment. He picked up her "I am not your Savior, Coffee IS!" mug and threw it with high velocity into the forehead of Kelly Granta, knocking her unconscious and propelling the letter out of her hand like a single ski from a fallen skier.

Section 2, Part III

Lucky

1

Start / Stop

His new partner, Abby, lived in a ranch-style home in an area which flooded, but companies would not offer flood insurance unless it was mandated, at a cost of over $10,000 per year. This pretty much summed up her life. Abby, often described as sensible, thought this made no sense. The house reminded her of the ranch her grandfather used to own, but his had a handicap ramp that wrapped itself around the side of it from the garage up to the front door. Wheelchair-bound, he still drove as he always did, the lack of mobility caused by a hunting accident when he was in his thirties. Grampy did pretty well for himself, given that challenge, reminding everyone that the only time he had been hindered was when the automatic garage door opener malfunctioned and he was stuck in there for three days until his wife came home from a trip. He ate canned goods that they had stockpiled in there, opening the cans with a knife he found in the garage near his workbench. The process was pretty simple, and it involved using the heel of the knife, the part next to the handle, like an old-school can opener. Abby received much of her own sensibility, and survival instincts, from her Grampy's DNA.

Yet, it didn't seem sensible to anyone that she and Jack up and left their area to move to New Jersey. It made sense to her. Even at the late age of forty, she needed to be emancipated from her overbearing and critical parents. Once her grandfather passed, she tried to give herself a reason to stay, but her therapist seemed to recommend she go as far away as possible. That was all the Abby she needed. No more toxicity needed to remain.

Toxicity also, shortly after, led her away from Jack. Jack wanted a nice big house there, one with ornate columns, and the smaller ranch, which was purchased with too much sentimentality, caused a lot of resentment. Soon after, she didn't even know why she had moved, and what she was doing with him, so he had to leave. She got the house and didn't even need him to buy her out. The ranch was hers. She had purchased most of it with the money her grandfather left her.

※ ※ ※

Abby had made some growth. She was able to set boundaries and toss away people who represented negative energy and who contaminated her survival senses. That was progress, but in terms of perfection, she was less perfect in needing to be with someone. Being alone was difficult to her, especially if she believed some of the things her mother said which weren't at all true. Lucky found her beautiful and perfectly average in all other ways. Perfectly. She was always the most beautiful person in the room to him, but she never believed him, only thinking she was not more beautiful than a single person, and trying too hard to make up for that in all other ways.

Lucky couldn't see what was so far beneath the surface, but he just felt comfortable, the same comfort he used to feel with Grace, her being easygoing, nonjudgmental. Abby made life better. Abby seemed like the glue that held him together.

Now with Grace, Lucky still wondered why things had gotten so off track with Grace. They were both self-reflecting, even when their narratives became unreliable. Once something was cemented into either of their heads it was difficult to remove. And, Lucky too, had something now cemented into his head. It was the auditory hallucination of Grace's angry voice which often occupied Lucky's head.

2
Anonymous

Lucky sat at the front of a room of filled folding chairs and began speaking. It had been raining all morning, and lightning flashed through the garden windows in the damp basement of the New Jersey church. His sponsor, Shawn, sat in the first row, approving everything by nodding at anything Lucky was saying which represented the good message of experience, strength, and hope.

He and Shawn met every Saturday to work on The Big Book together. Shawn was a wild man when he was using, and, now sober, was still loud and energetic. Shawn was a good sponsor, always available, even if his rapid-fire conversation, often changing swerving off subject, made Lucky not want to call him as often as requested. Besides giving him help, Lucky felt Shawn was a friend, and Shawn was trusted enough, during Lucky's 5th Step, that Lucky's father was alive, even though the information was covered automatically in sponsor-sponsee privilege as a secret Shawn was never allowed to tell. And Shawn, was the only person he ever told. Even Grace never knew, and Abby, though it was suggested that Lucky tell her, wouldn't know yet either.

The storm had begun when Lucky started. "Hello, my name is Lucky, and I am an alcoholic. I'm not here because I was ordered by a court, or a person, and there was no intervention by any friend or family. I did this on my own, with my life not being out of control. I just needed to stop, and I didn't know how to stop on my own. Things in place are pretty good. I drank before my marriage ended, and it only increased after. Me and my current partner have grown together. She would like to stop drinking, but she's not ready yet. Maybe she should be in these rooms, but that is her journey not mine. I have now nine months under my belt. My health is better. My attitude is better. And, I have such gratitude.

So here is how it all started for me. I always drank, and it was a part of my life. Seems that it was normal as everyone around me was involved in drinking. It all seemed very normal. It never affected me negatively, and everything always went my way, until one day it didn't. My health went bad, and my luck went south, but that wasn't because of alcohol. The cause of that seemed to be from my ex-wife Grace who also is no longer in my life. Don't get me wrong, she's a great human being, but she just caused these things to happen. I mean, why else would things change 180 degrees. I've concluded that she was a variable. My life is better."

People started to shift uneasily in their chairs, as his share went away on a tangent from alcohol. Shawn pointed to his head, to signal Lucky to be smart and stick to the story, but Lucky plowed forward. "Still, I decided to keep going, and being at Abby's house where we would sit and have beverages in the living room every day, wasn't functional. I believe there was something at work that brought me and Abby together. Maybe it was our love of dogs. Maybe it was our combined losses, but, certainly, when I saw the bounce of her hair when she turned after trying to claim my dog. I still remember that bounce, slow motion, the world almost stopping. Abby didn't need to tell me to stop drinking. That was Grace, but I was unwilling to listen to her. In a way, I've stopped because of Abby, and also for myself. My medical condition is under control—all is good."

A power-surge caused the lights to flicker and dim, before charging back up again to full illumination. The disruption was felt in the room, and Lucky paused for two full seconds, confused. Shawn attempted to whisper, but instead, in a loud voice said, "Keep going."

This caused another pause but also seemed to snap Lucky out of the previous one. "All of these things have improved. Abby has been my savior. She is such a calm and gentle influence, and what she has gone through makes me want to be there for her, because she has selflessly been there for me."

And suddenly there was Grace's voice in his head, always an angry contrarian, *But you're a liar!*

This too threw him, and he look around to see if anyone else heard it. "I just want to do things for her, I mean not for her. For Abby, not for Grace. Whether we are out walking, listening to music, or just sitting in the dark, watching TV, I feel whole around her." The room flashed harshly from two quick bolts of lightning, followed by loud booms that made the room shake.

"There is more than just me, more than my own influence on myself in the world when she is around. And, and we cook for each other...but both of us say we will never remarry, but I'm just having a feeling that there is always a maybe. I mean look at this, look at all these miracles." Lucky waved at the room. "Now that I believe in miracles."

How dare you! What you called luck in your own life, others would have seen as a miracle! You've been living on miracles your entire life, and then time was up! Guess what, it starts now! Grace yelled out to him, and only him.

Lucky stopped his talk and felt as if his head were tingling. Grace was not there, but he could hear her—loud, and clear. Confused, again losing his place. He longed to be in bed, away from her voice, lying next to Abby, her basic, somewhat sexy, soft, cotton pajamas pushing against him on his flank, his nose full of her scent.

A huge lightning flash caused the lights to flicker two, three, then four times, followed by the loudest thunderclap of the evening.

It starts now! Grace's voice screamed within the clap of Lucky's head, and Lucky, in front of a roomful of drunks, fell off his chair, shaking, and having his first grand mal seizure in nine months.

※ ※ ※

What the others in recovery observed with Lucky's pauses and breaks within his share was concluded as some bad public speaking caused by a medical event. Either that, or he was in the middle of possible relapse, the seizures caused by that. Then there was this new confusion within the room when he fell from his chair, and that delay where people didn't know if they should do something, only waiting to see if they had to. People froze, and the room had stopped for a second. There was also the pause of people who wanted to help, but didn't want the meeting to end. Certainly a 911 situation would have put a pause in their recovery. Shawn made the call.

Lucky was conscious, but couldn't speak, when the EMTs carried him up the stairs out of the basement, and he hoped this neurological setback was just a small blip on the radar, nothing which would form a pattern. Grace, thank God, was no longer speaking in his head. Today's incident didn't make sense to the conclusions he had made about the direction of his new life with Abby; rather, it seemed like a regression of his past with Grace seeping in, dumping him into the ER with another follow-up in his future. When he was able to speak, he told Abby not to come to the hospital because by the time she did he would be discharged, and she might as well just walk Manny and Bingo. Shawn would drive him home.

"It's going to be OK," Shawn said on the way home, and also, again, when he arrived, with Abby and the dogs waiting for him.

※ ※ ※

It just felt wrong to Abby that Lucky didn't remember that during an electrical storm, walking was out of the question. Manny wanted nothing to do with the thunder and lightning, only cowered in the corner until the medication kicked in. *How could he not remember that?* Instead of walking the dogs, she made some soup and sandwiches for Lucky and Shawn when they arrived, just in case they were hungry. Her experience with seizures was limited enough to know that all Lucky would want to do was sleep when he returned, so food probably wasn't needed. She made it anyway. Shawn took a sandwich for the road, while the dogs, who hoped for a handout, gave up and joined Lucky in sleeping. Abby sat at the table and ate by herself.

During the times he woke during the night, Lucky was grateful she and the dogs were there, even if she was in another room. Like the dogs, Abby had this quiet presence, which always felt reassuring to him, but if things ever went badly for her for any reason, Abby needed time to regulate, and she talked through her anger and frustrations aloud. At first this was alarming for Lucky, seeing the usual conflict-avoiding Abby he knew fly into a state of agitation and take a good couple of hours to calm herself. There was nothing he could do during those times. Like Jack, he would leave her to reduce the boil on her own, except with Jack her agitation in the end was directed at him and always simmered to boil and back again continuously, the water never evaporating. When she talked about him now, it was still difficult to bring her down from her anger. Even recounting the small issues, *he forgot the milk*, or *he said he would take in the trash but didn't*, would keep her stewing for days...venting it all to Lucky.

Lucky had seen this wrath directed toward him once, and it had to do with his drinking. She, of course, didn't have the problem, but when he, in the span of a week, passed out on the sofa, causing one of the overly patient dogs (neither dog would admit it) to urinate in the kitchen, followed by him absentmindedly leaving the gate open, causing both dogs to be out on the town, he was in her wrath. Hearing Abby's anger was a big reason he checked out Alcoholics Anonymous, and he did so without telling her. All he knew was that things seemed to be better, and he wasn't doing so many dumb things, and he didn't do the really dumb ones when he was sober. He wanted to keep things right with Abby, because even though he couldn't explain it, it seemed like she was the last chance he would have of being in a relationship. It was do or die with her, and he felt like a button hanging by a thread off of a coat. He was the button, and she was the coat not doing anything but being a comfort.

❄❄❄

After he napped on the couch, Abby walked over and joined him, sitting where his head had been so that he could rest it on her lap. Quietly, she stroked his hair as if she were flattening the silk pillowcase she rested her own head on at night. Her fingernails combed through his hair easily, not at all like when she brushed back through the more course, curly hair of her own.

"Tell me. What were you like as a child? Handsome, I bet." Abby asked.

"I don't know. I know I never felt ugly," Lucky said.

"Handsome, blond-haired kid with pale blue eyes. Only child. Spoiled, I bet," she said playfully.

"Spoiled? I don't think they had to spoil me. Everything just came to me easily. In fact, I never had to ask for anything. Even at Christmas, I never made a list, I just got everything I wanted."

Abby knew enough to believe him, but somehow wanted it not to be true. "Do you miss them?"

"Of, course. What kind of question is that? Why wouldn't I miss them?"

"I'm sorry. That was a dumb question. What I meant is that you've done all this on your own. Oh, I don't know what I'm saying."

"I mostly feel bad. Maybe if I had been more alert when I was driving that night, all of it could have been avoided. Maybe I could have avoided the truck. I've stopped wondering about the *what ifs* though. I'm just grateful for my own life. There are always two unyielding ways to look at things if you're going to be black and white about everything. I try to avoid that."

"Karma too, right?" Abby added. "I believe in scientific outcomes and results, but I believe in karma as well."

The word karma, irked Lucky. What was the karma around his parent's death? What was the good and evil? He knew that everyone didn't deserve to receive everything, but his fatigued brain felt like it was about to explode, like a light switch being turned on and off repeatedly. His nerve cells which communicate with each other through electrical activity had just recently stopped communicating, so Lucky's feelings were certainly justified. His brain activity had been disturbed, and now he was disturbed, but in a way, he had baited her.

"None of that is true!" he yelled, moving so abruptly that Abby's nails scratched the side of his face. "Ouch!"

This sudden mood change reminded Abby of Jack. She never liked his mood changes, which she felt were connected to her need to run from him. Run from the conflict. She didn't want to conclude then and there that he was going to be just like Jack, but her mind went there. She tried to justify that he was not feeling well after the seizure, but Lucky grasped his face where he had been scratched.

"Goddamn it!" he shouted, which propelled Abby to stand from the sofa, Lucky's head bouncing of the cushion. She looked at their dogs lying on two dog beds in adjacent corners of the room. It was funny how they did everything together. "Don't make me tell you to leave," she warned him, walking into the back bedroom, with Manny trailing at her heels. Bingo did not move.

3
All Apologies

Lucky slept for the next ten hours. Then he felt a little shame. Had he actually picked a fight with Abby? He was ready and rested and needed to apologize. He would not repeat the same mistake. The recent seizure, as all seizures, affected him mentally, made him react differently—shorter in fuse, and less logical. This apology was not going to be like any 9th Step Amends he had learned to do. After all, it was just a little blow up, and she should forgive him, with things going back to the way they were right before it happened. Like a seizure, this usually wasn't the case, but still, he had a need to be forgiven. Usually, his looks and soft eyes would allow this to happen, no questions asked, but Abby had just been through something herself, and forgiveness was not automatic, her trust needing to be re-earned again, and again. Abby created marks of digression, and when you built up three strikes, it was cause for you to be out. Eventually, she might soften, but she never forgot what happened. She would have rather thrown him out than wonder if this would be the last time he would snap. It made her feel weak.

Like Lucky, his dog Bingo also slept for ten hours. Dogs tend to follow what their owners do. Manny, on the other hand, paced to Bingo's bed and then Abby's room, back-and-forth. Dogs also can sense when things are amiss with their owner. Abby concluded that Bingo was, for once, not flanking Manny because of his loyalty to Lucky, and Lucky was down for the count.

Usually, Bingo and Manny were on their same dog schedule, sleeping when it was time to, eating at the same time, playing with each other when it was time to chase a ball or pull a tug-of-war dog rope. When you own two dogs, they are even walked at the same time. Abby often looked at the two dogs, thinking if only relationships between humans were this simple. *Keeping it Simple*, was a phrase Lucky had been using, but he was one of the least simple people she knew. Even though she had just seen it for the first time, his hair-trigger was now on her radar, and she was now like a dog's ears popping up to a familiar sound, like a can of food being opened. Once you experience some trauma, the way she had, you always can sense what is potentially harmful outside a circle, right before it moves directly inside.

Abby also didn't like that Lucky had purchased a gun and was building some sort of larger gun storage rack in the basement. The heavy-duty handgun he kept in the car "for protection" as he put it, could be slightly justified. Him keeping one in a car wasn't something she could wrap her head around. She was not a gun person, but who was she to prevent anyone else from owning one! The basement build was something she didn't understand. Lucky must have some reason for the oversized storage cabinet, which looked to be able to house more than a few large weapons. His demeanor suggested that he had thought this out, and it was going to be a hobby or to be used for another activity. Lucky's friend Shawn had guns, but he used them for hunting, and as far as Abby knew, Lucky had no interest in that. Lucky did purchase some strange novelty t-shirt with a picture of what looked like a Mother Superior holding a machine gun, with the words *Guns for Nuns* placed above that. When she questioned Lucky on the odd choice of a very Pro-gun garment, he just laughed and said he thought the shirt was hilarious.

Secretly, Abby felt a sense of dread when she looked at the almost completed rack, soon to house what Lucky lightheartedly referred to as Death Sticks. When he used that term, it sent a chill through her, and now she knew he was on strike one of his three strike at-bat. Instead of conflict, she kept this fear to herself, and when Lucky suggested they get away for a week, she agreed, knowing they needed a change. They were headed to Nashville.

4
Nashville

The trip to Nashville turned out to be the ideal escape. Resentments seemed to be washed away with music, at every little spot on the strip, which started at 10 AM and concluded at around 3 AM. Abby made sure they weren't out anywhere close to that late, because she wanted him to be well rested because of his seizures, but it seemed like the birds in Tennessee had their own shows to do, starting at around 5 AM. Lucky and Abby did touristy things too, such as the Parthenon, which was amazing, constructed inside and out identical to the one in Greece. The Grand Ole Opry was a disappointment, the Musicians Hall of Fame and the Ryman much more compelling than *that* tourist trap. At Musicians Hall of Fame, Abby looked beautiful, a cut above perfectly average, as she danced in and out of the purple haze from the fog machine at the Jimi Hendrix exhibit. Later that night, Band of Horses were at the Ryman. Abby knew their music, and Lucky was clueless, but he enjoyed how animated and excited Abby was at seeing them, grabbing his hand, kissing him and squeezing her arms around his waist.

The next day was just as good as the last. They started at one end of Broadway and walked all the way down Honky Tonk Highway, stopping in place-to-place to see a different singer-songwriter, all of them amazing. There was no cover to get in, but each one had a jar or a hat to collect tips. After they had seen three wonderful acts, Abby suggested to the next performer, she place her name somewhere on the stage, because no musicians were ever announced or had their names on any of the club's signs. Their names weren't even the chalkboard stand-ups on the street outside. Abby noted this to Lucky immediately after leaving AJ's Good Time Bar, having really enjoyed the artist but only remembering part of their name...Barbara *Something-or-other*. They avoided Kid Rock's bar because Lucky said, "The place wasn't Nashville, and seemed like bullshit," to which Abby added, "Kid Rock is bullshit."

"And what the fuck is a Big-A Honky Tonk Rock'n'Roll Steakhouse?" he asked.

"A bunch of bullshit," she said, as they both laughed from bullshitting about the bullshit.

At Second Fiddle, a man looking out of place between the tourists and the musicians on break, walked in and was immediately yelled at by the muscular, black-haired bartender to leave.

"He looks homeless," Abby said to Lucky.

"Looks that way."

"Still, that's a pretty shitty way to be treated since it's free for anyone to walk in the door," Abby said.

The bartender overhearing them, said, "Yesterday he stole the tip jar from the band. That's not OK. These bands struggle to make money."

"Well...," Abby tried to respond but was interrupted by the bartenders loud, "Hey!" directed at the man who still wasn't leaving. Abby got off her stool and took out a twenty-dollar bill, but the bartender was quicker, barreling past her to put hands on the man's thin red and white flannel shirt.

"I'm no worse than the rest of you!" said the man being hustled out, who was still in the bartender's grips, as the bartender looked over his shoulder at Abby, who had her twenty-dollar bill extended and was following them out the door.

"Don't give him that!" he barked at Abby, who could feel Lucky's presence right behind her.

"It's my money, and I'll do with it what I please!" she responded, as the man was being shoved out the door with Abby and Lucky right behind them. "And we don't need to stay here either," she added, as the bartender briskly shouldered past her in the opposite direction, his job with the homeless man finished.

"Here," she said to the man, when she reached him outside, giving him the twenty.

He nodded, "Thanks. By the way, there's a really good BBQ place real close on Broadway. I recommend it."

"Thank you," Abby said.

Later in the day they also got some free stuff at Bourbon Street Blues and Boogie Bar at Printers Alley, hats, t-shirts, visors,—Lucky making a face, wearing the visor backwards for a photo for Abby's iPhone. They looked so comfortable that a neighboring table offered to take a picture of them hugging, with the band in the background. Lucky lingered on the freshness of her hair which smelled of coconut conditioner. It was just a wonderful trip, with no need for any luck or lack of it to pull them through. Just he, and Abby, the world spinning all so perfect and gently on its axis at a time and place which could never be duplicated.

5

Heavenly Father

It happened the final evening of their perfect vacation when he received a call.

"I'm sorry to inform you, but your father has passed," was the first thing said to Lucky after the caller introduced himself.

Lucky and Abby had just finished making love at their hotel, and it was the disparity between this event and the news he received which stunned him more than expected. He blocked out some of the information he was hearing because it was too much to process.

"Yes. Yes. OK. Thank-you." Hang up.

Abby was stretching, lying on her back, her face moistened from the afterflow of their passion, a light sweat worked up from being on top of him. Lucky sat up next to the bedside table facing the opposite wall. After two minutes she finally asked, "Hey, what was that all about?"

"It was nothing," Lucky said.

"No, everything in your face just changed. What was that?"

He knew he had to tell her, and then his lie would be uncovered, but that was small in the realm of what was going through his mind right now. "My father died."

Abby was confused. "Why are you getting calls now? Are there still some things that were left not done. It's been how many—"

"No, he just died. He died today," Lucky admitted.

Now it was Abby's turn to be silent. *Why the hell would he not have ever told me that his father was alive?* She was livid, but right after him hearing this kind of news, she knew to not express that anger to him, "I don't understand."

"My father didn't die from the accident."

"OK?"

"He didn't. But he was injured in such a way that it would have been better if he had been. He died in a facility," Lucky said.

She hated how matter of fact he sounded, and quickly concluded that the held onto lie was to cover up the guilt and shame of what had happened, producing a fictious death so that he didn't have to be responsible for the past, present, and future of his father. He could just wash his hands of it all. This too made Abby fume.

"And you're just telling me this now?" She blurted out.

"There wasn't a need to let you know, so now, there is," Lucky said quietly, almost as if he didn't want her to hear, or he didn't want to hear it himself. He ran his hand through his long, blond locks and stroked his chin, catching the sandpaper feel of it on his thumb and pointer, thinking of other things he had kept hidden, such as Grace viciously occupying a voice inside his head from time-to-time. Abby slid over, and curled around his torso and extended buttocks. She was mad, but she also knew this must be extremely difficult for Lucky to be going through right now. She placed her arms around his waist, him still facing away from her, and he moved his large arms down to wrap the top of her forearms which held him tightly.

"Thank you, Abby."

She was still mad. "It's OK," she said.

6

Reflections Of

Besides the lie, which was strike two, by the way, Abby was having a difficult time with the fact that a potential life-partner could wipe his father from his life. Even if the accident was his fault, and even if his father was seriously injured, Abby was of the mind that a person with a serious head injury would still be able to sense the presence of a loved one. She thought about coma victims coming out of comas and without any scientific reason knowing things or conversations that had occurred when they were not in full attendance. *There are so many things about Lucky I like,* she thought, but all this new stuff puts things with him in a wait and see mode.

She thought of all of the things she *did* like about him. She knew she had to do this, so she started with the basics.

1) He was handsome.
2) He was charismatic.
3) If he wasn't being a good listener, he showed interest in her life and asking about it.
4) He had a great dog, and their dogs were buddies.

5) He was appreciative and grateful of her.
6) He was loyal.
7) He didn't give a shit about the relationship she just came out of.

Then she created a positive image of him looking at her over his shoulder, with his flowing blond hair, and now slightly gray, blowing in the breeze someplace on an ocean, his stubble defined and contrasted from the sun. She stopped short of listing all the things she did not like about him, because she wanted to keep the first list untarnished.

※ ※ ※

Lucky was reflective for the next couple of days, mentally preparing before he had to make the trip to the funeral home. That wasn't going to happen right away, but Lucky dreaded having to expose his poor financial situation to a total stranger. Of course, they would be sensitive, as they dealt with this all the time, he reasoned, but what kept him uncomfortable was mostly fear. He already planned to leave Abby at home when he conducted this business, because he also didn't want to reveal to her how little savings he had.

His life was full of what ifs. What if his life had no moments of incredible luck? What if there hadn't been an accident? What if he had visited his father, even in the condition he was in? What if he hadn't been married, because after all, what was rushed into with Grace was to force some sort of long-term connection in his life. After his parents, he didn't form many. Even with Abby, he felt somewhat disconnected, because he wanted to keep everything he had as his, including his secrets. His disconnections often put him in a place as dark as the black world within one of his seizures. 'Round and 'round it goes and how you might come out of it nobody knows. For that matter, what if he never had a seizure?

Although the decision to abandon what was left of his father was completely his alone, it helped him come to terms with another what if, the what if he had parents in his life? What if God had intervened and the outcome had been different? Lucky never had to go down that road, as his road was full of The World of Lucky, where everything worked out in the end, and also very well. But now, with the seizures, and a failed marriage, plus his father's death, he had a reason to doubt, and time to think. What kept coming to him was the scotch his father drank. Johnny Walker Black, with a black twist-off cap. Even the words sounded enticing. It would be quite a tribute to down a few, maybe to toast his father with Abby, in a safe, respectful way. He should probably call Shawn, as Lucky had not spoken to Shawn since his trip to Nashville, yet Shawn hadn't called him either, something he usually did when Lucky hadn't checked in, even for one day.

As the days clicked by, the idea of Johnny Walker circled in his head, complete with the ice-cubes swirling in his hand, going 'round and 'round. He reached for his phone to dial Shawn. It rang five times before it went to voicemail.

That's odd, Lucky thought, *usually he picks up.* Lucky wondered if Shawn was mad at him. He would give him another minute before dialing him up again, but suddenly the phone vibrated in his hand, startling him, and sending the phone to the ground.

"Hello," Lucky answered.

"Heeey, man," Shawn said.

"Hey, you sound sleepy," Lucky said.

"Hey, man, no. I'm sorry."

"That's OK, I'm glad you picked up," Lucky countered quickly.

"No, man," Shawn said, suddenly sounding more slurry than sleepy. "I've relapzed and am not in a good... a good...a good place right now. I sudzjest as your sponore, that you find another sponsor. Goodbye now."

The phone's screen in Lucky's hand went from brightly lit up to black, and suddenly he stood there with about as much of a defense against a drink as trying to prevent a phone's display from going dark.

7

Direct Communication

The twist-off metal cap on the fifth of Johnny Walker Black was being screwed off and on often, as if each time there were an actual decision made, but there was no debate and was no turning back, as Lucky sat in the garage downing glass after glass without any control. He had instantly progressed to the previous place in his drinking, and now, blacked out, he wasn't alone there. His eyes were glassy, and he was leaning against a wood beam on the wall hearing Grace's voice goading him on again. There was no thunder, no lightning, just the clear, perfect, tone of Grace's voice. He thought that this might be a precursor of another seizure, but he wasn't feeling the confusion or the aggressive way his mind went, almost craving sensory conflict, before a seizure began.

Grace was not kind voicing her commands. *Was she ever?* he thought. It was almost as if he was another one of his projects, like the kid in her high school class she told him about, with a disability, whom she mentored.

One of the directives was to go to Bingo's and get some guns for his gun rack. *Be careful, Twisty,* she said to him. *Remember you were going to buy one to kill ME.*

"Who is Twisty?" Lucky wondered aloud.

Twisty is the sick and twisted mind you have adopted, not to mention the twist off top, Grace's voice said.

"I was joking about the killing part," Lucky said.

Jokes, the voice said, *are things you say out loud to make other's laugh. You were not fucking joking.*

The warmth of the scotch made Lucky feel like he was in some sort of zone, locked into believing something that may or may not exist was able to send him messages. "OK, fine. It wasn't a joke, but how did you even know?"

I know everything. So, buy the gun and kill if you want—just don't kill me, OK? Because you will. You have to. You are down. Fucking do it. You have done nothing in your life, so you need to do this. Loser! Fucking loser, drunk again! Go buy your guns. Do it!

"Hunh?"

Do it!

Lucky heard one of the dogs let out a weak bark inside the house, so Lucky got up to have the dogs join him in the garage. Abby was not home, which was one of the variables for relapsing, so he half-expected both dogs to see and run up and jump up on him. Instead, the door hit something on the way to swinging open, and it was only Manny who ran to him. Bingo was lying on the floor, lethargic, and surrounded by diarrhea. His thoughts ran from when the last time he'd let Bingo out, to having to clean it up, to that his dog was sick. His thoughts went from these to knowing he had to do something. He felt he needed to call Shawn now, but he couldn't call Shawn. Shawn had resigned from being his sponsor because he was active again. Lucky knew that Shawn was drunk as well, but then again if they were both active the call could be made. *Did Shawn only want to be his friend as a sober person?* The question bugged him.

He dialed the number, and it rang a few times then went to voicemail. He immediately dialed it back, and the same thing happened. Bingo was still on the floor without much energy as Lucky slid his hind quarters away from the mess to towel it up. Lucky retched from the smell, which is perhaps one of the worst things that can happen when you have a belly full of booze that hasn't been full of booze in quite a while. He needed help—even if it was just to get Bingo cleaned up, but he knew, as much as he wanted to deny it away, that he was going to have to get him to the Veterinarian Hospital. Abby was the next call he was going to make.

Lucky delayed a few minutes. *Could he call her and not sound drunk?* Abby had supported his sobriety because Lucky was much more pleasant and motivated to do just about anything, as he was motivated to do nothing when drunk. *Would she be mad, and would that matter? I do have some sort of event going on here.*

Lucky wretched again.

Fuck, he thought, going to his recent calls and hitting the second one down without looking, assuming it was Abby, which was a pretty good assumption, as Shawn and Abby were the only calls he made or received of late, and he had just called Shawn. Lucky shoved the phone against his ear, and wondered with his current luck would the call go to voicemail the way it had with Shawn after four rings. Immediately after the fourth one, it picked up.

"Hello, hey, hey, hello," Lucky said quickly. "I have a problem."

"Um, hello," Grace's voice said, clear and clean into his ear, not like the angry voice that had occupied his head today. He had dialed Grace's number instead. This time the voice answered not yelling or distorted the way it sounded in his head.

"Grace??? Who is this, Grace?" he said, almost yelled into the phone, right before he fell to his knees and vomited. When he pulled the phone back up from where he was holding it pinned against the floor, no one was on the other line. Then he left the dogs at home; got in his car; and drove to Bingo's Bing-Bang Gun Shoppe. "Go buy your guns," he said out loud.

8

A Perfect Storm Starting

Lucky thought to use his credit card to buy an AR-15 at Bingo's Bing-Bang Gun Shoppe without any wait period. The man in charge, Barry, looked, as Lucky suspected he would look, like he was going on a hunting trip—fatigue jacket, orange hat with flaps. Hidden underneath, which Lucky couldn't see, was a *Guns for Nuns* t-shirt, now the #1 Top-selling article of clothing for gun lovers in America. There were some other things also hidden. The first was when Lucky asked for a 'Bazooka', which was code for extra payment for a same day, no permit required, purchase. This went fine, except Barry shushed him when he used the code word. The gun was produced. The second was when Barry asked if he were intoxicated, and Lucky said, "No." Barry didn't really have to ask because he could smell it on Lucky as quick as the hanging bell on the front door rang upon opening. None of that mattered because Barry saw he drove a BMW, and that was something which vouched for his character.

The third thing hidden had to be Lucky's credit card. Barry said that when buying a 'Bazooka' it is traceable via credit card. Barry directed Lucky to the closest ATMs for cash advances. Barry told him the cost it was going to come to for a semi-auto AR pattern sporting riffle. It was $1000 for the rifle, plus a $1,000 expediting fee, and of course Lucky calculated the additional $50 for each of the cash advances. Barry also told him that his gun's serial number would be cleaned so the gun would be untraceable. *It doesn't matter. You don't want to be traced, and, in fact, nothing matters*, he heard Grace's voice say in his head. *Well, what are you waiting for. Go!*

Lucky had only one credit card he could use that wasn't useless, and triumphantly walked out of the third ATM vestibule, finally with enough money he needed and headed back to Bingo's.

"Fuck you," he said out loud to invisible Grace, as a customer at Bingo's overheard his profanity backed away from him, the ball of rage. Barry completed the transaction. Service with a smile.

Behind the wheel of his BMW, he saw Abby's car in the driveway. She was standing outside an open front door. As Lucky drove closer he saw she was crying. *Damn,* he thought, she must have found the empty bottle in the garage, *but crying? That's a bit dramatic.* He shook his head quickly from side to side, trying to shake off his inebriation, and displayed the biggest smile he could create, just so that she might fall for how well things were in the world.

"You weren't home? Did this just happen?" Abby sobbed.

"Yes, sorry," Lucky answered.

"Sorry??? You left him there?"

At first Lucky thought she was referring to Barry. *Now why would Barry come with me?* was his initial flawed thought.

"Let me explain," Lucky said, trying to figure out on the fly what he needed to explain first. What did Abby know? Was he explaining the relapse, tje driving drunk, or was he explaining the gun purchase?

"And Manny. Manny is beside himself!" Abby yelled.

When she mentioned Manny, the rush of the memory of his dog lying in his own watery waste came back to him. "Oh my God," he said. "I was just out trying to buy something that would help...looking for an Anti-diarrhea pill for dogs? Imodium for dogs? Look, I couldn't find any."

"It's too late," Abby snapped through her tears. "Bingo doesn't need anything anymore."

9
Hotel Happening

The room had the clean, yet stale, smell that most chain hotels have. He was placed in a non-smoking room, but the room faintly seemed to have an old odor from the smoking which had gone on in it. The bedspread was green with brown and pink flowers, the carpet blue-gray, and the two lamps affixed to the wall were perfectly equidistant from each side of the bed. The headboard was mounted on the wall, not attached to the frame for ease of who knows what. Looking up from the pillow at a place he didn't know, the television was on and annoying him with South Park reruns, probably the worst sounding program to hear when you come to. There was a Sonic bag by the nightstand, saturated with a large spot of grease at the bottom. No water could be found within arm's reach, and God, did he ever need water. There was an empty bottle of Johnny Walker there instead, certainly within reach.

Handfuls of colorful brochures were scattered on the floor. They were tough to make out, but typical exciting looking photos on the front with yellow and red slanted large font that pronounced. "Visit the Grand Ole Opry" or something to that extent.

"How did they get here?" Lucky said aloud, running his thumb and pointer down his chin. *I must have had it in my suitcase from our trip?* he thought recalling the vacation that had just happened but seemed to have taken place forever ago.

Then, Lucky got a flash of memory, this one seemed very concise. Lucky was recalling holding the semi-automatic rifle in his hands, and an angry Abby telling him that he had to go, yelling at him that he had to get his shit together. He had no recollection of much of anything after that real-life movie ran through his head. *The gun. The gun. Where the fuck is the gun?* he thought. *And did I do something? Fuck.*

He put on a pair of shorts, and a t-shirt, stained with ketchup, the only one he could find, and walked past the lobby and into the parking lot. The blacktop felt rough but also cool and wet on his bare feet as it seemed to have rained recently. His car was not immediately visible, so it took Lucky a few minutes to find it, but he did manage to avoid the ground glass in between rows of cars. When he hit the remote to pop the trunk, to his relief, the gun was out, lying over the spare tire, and the ammunition was still unopened, indicating the gun hadn't been fired. Then on the way back to the hotel, he noticed all the license plates from other cars he walked past were from different states, which didn't strike him too much as odd, because after all he was at a hotel, but when he walked past the van used for the hotel shuttle space, the plate read, "The Volunteer State" and the side of the vehicle proclaimed, "The Nashville Express." At the desk he asked for a newspaper, and he was handed a copy of *The Tennessean* and *Ah, fuck, I am in Tennessee,* popped into his head. Upon checking the date, he saw that he had been there for 3 days. Then he checked his phone, with multiple outgoing calls to both Shawn and Abby which hadn't been returned. He knew Shawn had relapsed, but he was upset Abby didn't pick up. After his clearing the recent call list, there still was a red notification on the phone icon, which said there was a voicemail. There were several voicemails, one from Abby which hadn't been listened to and was 2 days old, and fifteen or so from Drake's Funeral Home. Apparently, he had answered one of the calls, and based on her voicemail he'd given them Abby's number.

I want you to stop calling me, and I want you to come back and get your stuff. What you did was scary, and even if you sober up, I can't be around it anymore. This was not what it was when things started. I've given you chances, and I just can't trust you anymore. Also, the Funeral Home keeps calling as if I can do anything about that. Let me know when you are planning to do this so Manny and I won't be around.

He called her number, and she didn't pick up. He called Shawn's number, and he didn't pick up either. Then back to Abby's number, this time leaving a voicemail apologizing profusely and asking for forgiveness. He knew that this message was sincere and honest, and if Abby could sense that sincerity, maybe everything would go OK. Halfway through the message, Lucky's voice cracked, but he kept on leaving the message, while crying, thinking that he might never have the chance to hold her again, or kissing her passionately, and that he was the reason he might never see her ever again. It was less than two weeks before Christmas, a holiday that multiplies one's loneliness by about a million times.

10
Shooter

Physically, Lucky felt awful, but upon counting his pills, he felt he had been responsible enough to take his seizure medication every day. All of this, he knew, was a new bottom. He had heard about other's bottoms during AA meetings, but he never considered his to be as bad as theirs, but as Shawn used to say, "If you're bottom isn't deep enough, you can always grab the shovel and dig yourself deeper." How true.

On the way back to New Jersey, Lucky was sure to drive carefully. Being pulled over as an unregistered gun owner, a semi-automatic rifle without a serial number in his truck, would disrupt all the plans he had been making. Things could go in various directions, but at this point, Lucky was going for redemption by earning forgiveness from Abby, burying his father, and even saving Shawn.

The drive back to Jersey would take around fourteen hours. Lucky could not imagine how he managed to drive to Tennessee in a total blackout and remain in that state for the time he had. He didn't know if he even made it in one full sweep behind the wheel.

He had planned his first stop to be at Abby's to present a case which would soften her. Worst case scenario was she would tell him off and he would have to make a case to get some clean clothes out of the house. No guarantees about any of this. Then he would go to Shawn's, no matter what happened at Abby's, just to check in on his former sponsor and friend. If he never asked for another sponsor, then was Shawn still officially a former sponsor, and if Shawn had worked his way back toward recovery, would he be back to being his actual sponsor? And if Shawn were still active in his alcoholism, certainly Lucky understood the primary purpose of helping another alcoholic. Lucky was feeling like the old luck he used to have would make everything work, and he was beginning to nudge a bit out of his darkness and toward hope.

Not so fast, Twisty, Grace mocked him in his head. *You still have some dangerous issues in that dark little head of yours. Use them at your discretion.*

11

The Road to the Road to

The door to Abby's was locked, and Lucky's keys no longer worked. Lucky waited a few hours in the dreary and cold December day before he dozed off in his car. Lucky suddenly jumped, awakened by a police officer rapping at the driver's side window of the BMW. Officer Meloncon was stocky, but mostly from the bulletproof vest she had on underneath her blues. To Lucky, Lorraine Meloncon didn't look like anyone someone would want to mess with, but he still wondered why she was out on a call without anyone with her. *Abby must have come by while I was asleep and called.* This could lead to the worst-case scenario involving the gun in his trunk, but fortunately for him, all Officer Meloncon wanted was him to move on.

"The owner doesn't want you on the premises," she told Lucky.

"Yes, Ma'am," he answered, reading her name tag. "I thought as much, Officer," giving her a smile worth a million dollars, while his mind stayed occupied with what was in his trunk. *Give her no need for to ask for it to be opened.*

He gazed at her name tag. "What does the *L* stand for? Lucy?"

"Do you have somewhere to go? Officer Meloncon is fine."

Lucky thought, *Well yes, I am going to go to Shawn's, but I don't really have a place to go,* but instead said, "Yes, Ma'am."

"There are some hotels up the road if you need directions," Office Meloncon said, pointing out to the end of Abby's driveway.

"You know I used to live here. I think I can find them," he answered.

As Lucky pulled away, he noticed her patrol car following him, about 100 yards back. He took the ramp to the highway to brush her off, driving to the next town as promptly as possible.

Exiting the highway, Lucky was alone again. He didn't want to confront Abby, but he did want to know what was going on, and when he dialed her number, she answered, "Having the police there isn't a good enough hint that I don't want to see or talk to you?"

"How was I supposed to know that?"

"Maybe our last confrontation isn't fresh enough in your mind? It's fucking pretty fresh in mine," Abby said.

"Do you want to meet up somewhere? I don't know, have dinner?"

"No."

"Maybe a drink? I won't be drinking, but you can have one."

Abby found the suggestion to be completely tone-deaf, and she let out an audible gasp, not knowing how she should respond to something so obvious to her, but not to him.

"Look, I gotta go," she said and hung up, solving it.

Lucky immediately dialed her back, but she would never again pick up a call from him from this point on.

※ ※ ※

Another person who hadn't answered him in a while had been Shawn, but Lucky felt their relationship wasn't troubled like the one he had with Abby, so dropping in wouldn't be much of an issue. They used to meet 1:1 to study the Big Book and work on recovery. When Lucky pulled into Shawn's house, he saw Shawn's older BMW in the driveway. This was a good sign. He was always amused that they drove the same make of automobile, though Shawn's was older, the paint's glimmer flattened from the years sitting in the sun. Also, some of the bells in his own car may have drifted out of tune, and the whistles were missing the triller balls.

Shawn had a good life. He worked, and lived with Monica, who was very attractive. Monica always would say hello then retreat to another room, out of sight, her long, straight hair dancing with each step. Shawn had told him that after such a long time, Monica was one of the gifts of the program. Every meeting, Shawn served Lucky an omelet, toast, and coffee if it were morning, and sandwiches for lunch if they got together later.

"The Big Book does happen to say that the women should serve the men at the meeting coffee and sandwiches, but that's kind of sexist, don't you think," Shawn once said while placing a Cuban sandwich in front of Lucky. "And to think the powers that be are so frightened to change even a single word in this book."

"Why not?" Lucky asked.

"Because it's worked so well as-is, people are scared."

"Kind of like the Bible," Lucky said.

"Well...."

Lucky always liked the back and forth he had with Shawn. Shawn always seemed so normal, a regular person who happened to be in recovery. He looked forward to the days they'd get together.

Somehow, this time, as he approached, it felt different. Lucky concluded that maybe it was because the weather had been overcast all day, or maybe he didn't know what he was walking into with Shawn. Either Shawn was going to be drunk, hungover, or in early days of recovery, ironically, like the same way Lucky felt. Also, he hadn't even spoken to Shawn; he was just dropping in, at a different time from their usual meeting time. Lucky was prepared to deal with all these variables.

Lucky rang the bell. Nothing happened. He heard no footsteps, no "Just a minute," people usually yell from behind a door. Just when he turned to walk away, he heard the doorknob turn and the screen door unlatch as it was pushed open. Lucky felt relieved that Shawn, even answering the door late, which was not a good sign, was home. But when he turned around, it wasn't Shawn. Monica was standing in the doorway, wrapped in a large fluffy bathrobe, opened semi-widely above the waist. Lucky felt strange that there was nothing at all sexy about how she looked, her face appearing sallow.

"Monica?"

Monica stood not moving or forming words until Lucky took a step toward the door.

"You've not heard," she said without any inflection. Lucky didn't assume anything, but it didn't seem as simple as that he was in rehab.

"No," he answered.

"He seemed to be doing well, and he told me he was going to go fishing early in the morning. He even took his stuff that morning." Monica's voice stayed undramatic and robotic as she told Lucky the story, and Lucky recognized that it was a voice flattened out by trauma, the after-effect of days of crying. "He called me, and said he had been hit in the head, and was lying down in some basement. I kept asking him where, and he couldn't tell me. All he said was that he hit his head, and that he had called the police, but he had no idea where he was."

"Was he...is he alright?" Lucky cut in, but Monica just continued, almost tediously plowing through.

"So, I hung up and I called the police. I gave them his phone number, so that they might ping his phone to locate, but they said they couldn't do that, but, in a few hours, they found him anyway."

"Is he OK?" Lucky asked.

"No, they found him. It was too late."

Though Lucky anticipated that this was the way the story was headed, he was not prepared for it at all. He had hoped that maybe Shawn was OK, even in a coma or something, but certainly, not dead.

"Too late? What do you mean too late?" he asked.

"I'm sorry. I don't know what else to tell you. I don't know what to do. The service is going to be in a few weeks. The police have his phone—I think had an autopsy done, but they won't tell me anything. There is an investigation."

The steps, the door, and Monica were now spinning. Lucky knew that this wasn't going to turn into a seizure, but rather it was his body's physiological reaction to a loss, and all his other losses. He gripped the thin metal handrail as he stepped within arm's reach of Monica, at the top of the steps, who hugged his head in her arms, and said once more, "I don't know what to do."

"I'm sorry," Lucky said. "I'm sorry. I won't, I can't—I will not be around for the funeral," and like a bolt of lightning, almost as if he had no control over what he was about to say, blurted out, "I'm moving to Tennessee." Then thinking what he had in his trunk, "I have everything I need."

12

The Theme from M*A*S*H*

The version of Theme from M*A*S*H* from the movie had lyrics. Lucky must have seen the television show a million times when he was a child, but inside the cabin at Abe Martin Lodge and Cabins, ten minutes outside of Nashville, the movie was on, which he had seen for the first time with Abby, months earlier. Lucky related to the scene in which Walter "Painless Pole" Waldowski was given a sleeping pill, thinking that he was in for an assisted suicide, but how the group had tricked him. Private Seidman sung *Suicide is Painless* during The Last Supper scene...amazing that in the middle of The Korean War, guitars can be found readily to be used on occasions such as this.

At Abby's, she knew all about it. She knew a lot about a lot of useless, yet extremely interesting things. The movie's theme song was scored by Johnny Mandel, and Director Robert Altman, as part of the deal, wanted the song's lyrics to be the stupidest imaginable. He even tried to write the lyrics himself, but he wasn't successful in writing something *stupid* enough, so he gave the task to his fifteen-year-old son, who wrote it in five minutes.

Someone that knew interesting useless facts was someone he could love forever, through any of their faults. But she, like the rest, did not have any more love for him, but he missed her anyway. He missed that life, with a dog, and a faraway father, going to meetings and having a sponsor. They were recent losses, fresh wounds, which if they happened further apart, he could have *one-day-at-a-timed* them to self-care. But they didn't, and he was shit out of luck with a boatload of pain. Suicide, he hoped, was painless because the pain of that would be much less than the pain of living.

And what was that pain? Lucky had a list. The pain of caring when it turned out it didn't matter if you cared at all. The pain of loss of this was something major. The pain of causing pain. The pain of having no one to turn to because people had left him to his own accord. The pain of being alone on the holidays. Also, that voice in his head being louder than his own thoughts, making him think he was crazy. *Grace, Abby, Bingo, Shawn, Grace, Abby, Bingo, Shawn.*

Do it! the voice now yelled. *You already killed your father. You tried to kill Abby. You wanted to kill me. You don't want to remember any of it!*

The gun in his trunk wouldn't do. Too messy and potentially painful. The sheer power of the gun could blow his head off, which was the best-case scenario.

He wished he had enough pills to drift away, but Abe Martin himself warned him other folks staying on the grounds may just pop in, or knock or the door, or do something which would interfere with this final goal. He had heard knocking at his door a few times in the five days he had been here, and he had brushed them off, staying under the covers, thinking the worst of himself, just waiting, waiting for a good time to end it all. He wanted to end his life but hadn't the guts. Then he again heard the voice that had followed him from New Jersey, *Suicide by cop!* it shouted. *Get the fuck out of bed and scout the area! You can hunt now. Hunt the tourists, and remember they are no better than you are. This will solve your problems. You think you could get me, but you can get them and also end your own miserable fucking life! Do it!*

The remanent voice of Grace stayed in his head for the rest of the day, and then the next, and the next, in longer and more urgent messages than ever before. It was impossible to sleep, and the constant barrage was weakening him, making him think that listening to the voice was more and more a good idea, or at least, the thought was, it would end the voices.

Section 2, Part IV

Bobby-Joe

1

Acceptance Speech

Bobby-Joe Malone's acceptance speech hit all the talking points. He was an expert in this area. He praised the *Guns for Nuns* group, stating they were not responsible for his wife's shooting. He mentioned that if a gun was reachable, the killer wouldn't have had a chance, but as you know, "Liberals are big on taking our guns away. The hero we needed, which could have kept my wife alive, was disarmed!"

Also, there was the issue of mental health. "We need more mental health programs that can keep people like that off the streets," Bobby-Joe stated candidly. "In my term here in office, I will advocate for stricter mental health policies and a promise of wellness. Why do we need extra screening to purchase a gun, which is our Second Amendment right! If we restrict access to society for those who are suffering from delusionary thinking, they will be the ones not able to walk into a store and buy one, and the people that can walk in, you'd better believe that they have earned that right, that they are safe and good people who do not need to be locked up. We still don't know who killed Candace, but someone like that wouldn't be able to get away if they were already put away! That is one thing Candace Malone got wrong."

Bobby-Joe's winning campaign was fueled on two strong doctrines. One was him being a sympathetic character, and the second was even after the tragedy, he was still all-in for gun rights. The NRA was proud to have him speak up for them, in fact it was a paid endorsement. Right after the assassination of his wife, they met with Bobby-Joe; briefed him on the agenda; and asked if he was willing to accept a quarter of a million dollars a year to talk about truth, justice and the American way, which was all to be endorsed through under-the-table payments. And if his political career expanded in the future, was he willing to continue to be a champion of the Second Amendment?

Bobby-Joe met these stipulations with a resounding, "Yes!" None of it was a stretch to Bobby-Joe's belief system, and what made it easier was that there was no information on the shooter, such as where he purchased his guns, and what he, the shooter, believed in. It made it easy for him to just talk about how his wife's assassination wasn't based anything at all on guns, but, rather, it was mental health that was needed to be cracked down on.

Juliet Debrusk wasn't a supporter of the two main pieces of Bobby-Joe's gun agenda. For one, Candace had let on that Bobby-Joe's belief system was different from hers. She used his in order to get her into office, but he used his because he truly believed it. Seeing Bobby-Joe speak after he won the seat made her first angry, then upset, and finally, sick to her stomach. She saw how much support he was receiving and knew she was up against a much stronger force than Candace Malone, one that could use his political power for all kinds of personal gain, both career and financial. Candace's death also, besides killing Juliet's momen-tum, was something that re-traumatized her. It brought her back to her own helplessness around Ophelia, and when popular opinion didn't allow to feel *that,* then she must be the bad one. It was outrageous, but the public gaslighting her on Twitter was about a million people against one, her, and she was not that strong.

Logically, Juliet thought, the man's own wife was killed in broad daylight. Certainly, decreasing the availability of guns would decrease cases like this. Certainly, someone with the flawed mental capacity to do this might be screened out in the gun-buying process. Why won't people understand the complete and utter logic of something like this? Did they have to lose someone? Losing Candace Malone seemed more powerful to her than losing Ophelia, even if the devastating pain around the loss of her daughter would never go away, nor was she expecting it to. Lobbying had helped distract her from this, but now that too had been taken away from her.

And there he was, in her face, full of himself, in an expensive-as-shit suit, positioned in front of a green screen, full of the skyline of Nashville, which he helped build, praising his opponent, Ken Sannison, whom he had just beat. Bobby-Joe's political career, like his suit, sure looked good on him. Bobby-Joe took the money and the votes from the NRA gun lobbyists, and he certainly earned it.

2
No Comment Which Has Any Meaning

Unlike the person that previously held his seat, that being his wife Candace, Bobby-Joe Malone avoided commenting on every gun incident which drew national attention. "No comment," could be interpreted as crass, which is what the results of a focus group study confirmed. Even though Anti-gun people mocked the "Thoughts and Prayers," rhetoric, it was a safe, useful, while at the same time, a useless, thing, to say. Malone's voter base, according to a focus group study thought that thoughts and prayers were perfectly reasonable to request during times of great need. The participants all agreed that there are infinite circumstances in which thoughts and prayers could be useful, and especially scoring high with the focus group was the value of "they couldn't hurt."

Smack in the middle of the gun debate, Bobby-Joe Malone and the memory of his deceased wife were not viewed as gods, Jesus, or even martyrs. Bobby-Joe and Candace were concluded by the study as red, white, and blue, Americans, championing and dying for what they believed in, and what they truly believed in was being voted into office and staying there by whatever means possible.

※ ※ ※

Matthew and Mary Taylor had comments. They felt proud of their daughter, as she did whatever it took to succeed, but now that she was dead there was no reason for the Taylor's to hold onto their beliefs, the ones that helped get their daughter elected. It was inconceivable to them that someone could walk up to their successful daughter and put a bullet into her head, regardless of if she had changed her views. It was disgusting to them that her husband, Bobby-Joe, continued to spit out these beliefs. How strange it was to see Bobby-Joe happy and celebrating while they couldn't see the end of their grieving. They alternated emotions; sickened, angry, and extremely sad constantly. Today it was anger. They were angry the killer was never caught and that the people in Candace's political party acted as if there were nothing which could have been done and nothing in the future could prevent this. So, they decided to speak at an Anti-gun rally in Nashville, to speak out against some "obvious" conclusions that American society defended. Against the warnings they heard regarding their own safety, they were going to speak on behalf of the life of their daughter Candace Malone.

3

Backward

Once upon a time, in a place close to your home, people loved God, and Jesus, a man who showed love and humility to everyone.

1) 1) Jesus was incredibly compassionate. You saw him time and time again responding to the needs of the suffering.
2) Jesus's respect for all of life was universal.
3) Jesus was an extraordinary listener. Whether it be his enemies or his disciples, Jesus valued people by listening to them and responding thoughtfully and patiently.
4) Jesus spent a great deal of time encouraging people towards love.

The people loved Jesus, the man, for all the above reasons, but those days are long gone. Now they loved men like Bobby-Joe Malone.

Bobby-Joe Malone: A man who never read the Bible but was willing to walk down Broadway with a worn Bible in his hand, while counting the votes the same way traditional politicians placed their hands to shake the hands of potential voters. True Believers are found where you look, and you shouldn't look in the media or in political campaigns. God and Jesus without manipulation for political gain had left us forty-plus years ago. Ronald Reagan rode on this, as did George H. W. Bush, and George W. Bush's "God Bless America," which closed out every goddam speech after 911, was not missed by people like Bobby-Joe Malone. *God Is My Lobby* is a powerful weapon when used by the wrong people. The facts were that Bobby-Joe Malone and the memory of his deceased wife may have been created in God's likeness, but in reality, they hadn't acted as Jesus would have at all, but perhaps Candace might be considered a martyr like him. Bobby-Joe made a point of promoting that. Bobby-Joe and his late Candace, the red, white, and blue, Americans, championing and dying for what they believed in, and what they believed in was being voted into office and staying there by whatever means possible.

Amen.

Section 3
The Shooter

1

Lucky

Help is available. Dial 988. Lucky dialed the number, but he wasn't sure what kind of help he needed. Not hearing the voices or wanting to kill himself would be a start. That would be a definite start.

They put him on hold.

"If this is an emergency dial 911," the voice told him. It was a voice that wasn't Grace's. *Yes, of course, I'm on the phone*, he thought as the recorded voice was replaced by a soothing yet unidentifiable melody, then back to the recorded voice message, and then the music-over-and-over-and-over, and back-and-forth, and back-and-forth, until the call was picked up.

A new voice that came on was a man named Tucker. Having Tucker interrupting the music was jarring to Lucky.

"Hi, how can I help?" Tucker asked.

"I don't know what to do," was Lucky's response.

"Tell me more about that."

"I'm drunk, and I want to kill myself. I'm hearing voices in my head of my ex-wife...and my dog died...and my girlfriend left me...my dad—,"

"Hold on a sec," Tucker said.

Lucky felt he needed to continue with his mental list. "You got all that...oh, and Shawn died too. He was my sponsor."

"Unh-huh," Tucker said.

"And I don't know what to do," Lucky said.

"What do you think you should do?" Tucker asked.

"Aren't you supposed to tell me?"

"I'm not a pro. You should seek a professional."

"What is 988 used for, then?" Lucky asked, as the world spun slower, suddenly halted.

"It's for getting things off your chest," Tucker said.

"So, you can't help me, tell me to not kill myself or fix anything? What if I might harm others?" Lucky asked.

"No. We are not professionals. You can talk about those things. Talk."

"What are you offering? So, what about wanting to kill myself?" Lucky asked, realizing that he wanted to kill himself less by talking to Tucker, mostly because he wanted to kill *him*.

"911," Tucher repeated.

"Hunh?"

"You can call 911. I mean, we're just here so people can get things off their chest. We really don't do too much except listen. Maybe you can take a walk, or—,"

Lucky hung up on Tucker in mid-sentence. Help is available, but apparently not for mental health needs. His semi-automatic was in his sightline but somehow the set-up and the mess if he used it on himself were overwhelming to him. Also, Lucky had some flawed logic still left over from Grace that told him the gun was bought to punish others. It was never intended for any other purpose. He had plenty of pills he could take, and if that wasn't enough, he could try to score some downtown. He didn't think that would be such a difficult thing, but first, where were the pills he already had?

What if he just took a walk, which Tucker suggested, maybe bring the gun, and maybe see what he should do? Just when he turned to dig through the mess of his room, he remembered what Abe Martin had told him, and he realized there hadn't been a knock on his door in at least a few days.

2

The Walk

It was windy, cold, and drizzly when Lucky walked toward the downtown area, his hair feathering around his pulled-up hoodie as if it were fake and glued to it. He had decided on an order of things. The gun would stay close, in his car, while he tried to find enough opiates to make it look like an overdose. He had parked far enough away so he could walk a bit, not to clear his head, but to increase the likelihood that he might suspect someone who might be holding or lead him in the right direction. If this didn't work out, then there was a possible death-by-cop scenario, which Grace screamed at him as being a viable idea.

Lucky was able to look down from a higher elevated area of Nashville down Broadway, which usually felt abuzz; the sunshine, signs, and bustle at all times of the day would leave no one to conclude anything but the best possibilities for the day. But today was gray, drizzly, and the people seemed to be of muted intensity because of the weather. Maybe it was muted because of his own suffering. Nashville's diminished beat was projected into his own thoughts. He saw a smallish group gathered around Broadway—conglomerated together like a dark, round spot or bullseye. Perhaps it was some political rally. Whatever it was they seemed like they were standing out for some reason.

As he reached this clarity, he was fully expecting Grace to yell something, but surprisingly, she was missing in his head at this moment, because at this moment he seemed uber-focused. What exactly did this sudden lack of guidance and new focus mean? Hadn't Grace led him down this track, and now that he could take a breath, he wondered why he was even here at all—which created once more the checklist of losses. Suddenly, he realized what his objective was, as a figure near him was just a movement caught in his peripheral vision. He, about 500 yards away, was now directly ahead of Lucky.

Get the gun! Get the gun! Grace yelled, and Lucky looked down to Broadway, knowing he needed to follow Grace's order. He should turn back to his car and do what Grace wanted and get it.

No! Get the gun! Get the gun! Grace yelled again, and Lucky looked down at the man, wondering who exactly would become the victim here if it all played out.

3

They Do Not Ring Out (Lucky's Reprieve)

Shots do not ring out, they pop. Just when Lucky walked toward the man, he heard them. Whoever says *ring out* never has been in an outdoor area with gunfire raging, cursing God for the unfortunate location they are presently in. Lucky was in it now. Anyone who knows anything about the sound of gunfire will describe it as a pop, like small fireworks, which Lucky was now successfully deciphering.

Fireworks? Some kids involved in a prank? No. Lucky knew what it was. The denial that it was something other than what it was quickly overruled, because why would people be running crazily in downtown Nashville if it were just a string of firecrackers the size of a pack of cigarettes? *Pop-pop-pop.* Lucky quickly discovered where it was coming from. The shooter was now in his sightline, not just a movement off to the side. Lucky was surprised the shooter was not wearing black military garb, or a heavy bulletproof vest. He should be dressed the same way a member of a SWAT team would be when defending people from a man such as this, armed with a semi-automatic. He is just wearing a red t-shirt and jeans, with a well-worn fatigue-patterned hat, long, uncut hair dangling well past the sweatband. Certainly, it was not a hat of a Major League baseball team.

Lucky was the only person anywhere near him, as all the other people were at a distance. There was no parting of the Red Sea of people falling like bowling pins, with people falling at a distance from Lucky and him. The shooter had not seen Lucky yet. The other people were a distance away and not safe. Sitting ducks.

Pop-pop-pop.

It is just my dumb luck that I'm in this position, the one with me and him, Lucky thought. *What happens if he turns around and shoots me. Will it be quick? Will it hurt? Maybe, if I'm lucky, it will just blow my head off. What happens if he does? Do I really not give a fuck? Should I? I've been wanting that outcome, so no harm, but as far as my own plan for this: Definitively foul. I certainly didn't want it to go down THIS way.*

Again, Lucky's recent life flashed before his eyes, making his thoughts more concrete. People swirled around circular: his father, Grace, Bingo, Abby, and Shawn.

They're all gone. Who is left to miss me. I will not be missed. Lucky told himself the way he had told himself so many times recently, after Grace intervened and before 988 was called. *Things never change, and there isn't any help.*

People often suggest that talking about it helps. What always stopped Lucky were those thoughts were so hard to explain to others, even therapists, who knew patients just cover up the really hard stuff they need to work on. Lucky suddenly remembered a friend who committed suicide forty-or-so years ago, and his now eighty-year-old parents were still trying to explain it. They are trying to find the answer, still trying to crack the case. Even with help, he knew depression and thoughts of negative self-worth would just pop up, as they have. He'd never acted on them, never sought help, because now it was today, and today was *still* happening.

Lucky's main discomfort now was the wind and drizzle. There would be no case to crack, the possible outcomes obvious.

He still doesn't see me, Lucky thought, as the shooter walked toward Broadway, the rounds ricocheting off buildings, cars, and striking some people in the distance, none of them knowing what hit them. Chaos which began with *pop-pop-pop*, a sound now mixed in with a sustained din of screaming between firings. *I can escape with my life, but there is nothing left for me to lose, just my life, and if I succeed this shooting is stopped, and if I fail, then my life is over...and so what? There's no risk there, and there are people on the street to whom intervention might mean something. They are sons and daughters, husbands and wives, people who are important to other people.*

Lucky quickly worked through another mental check in, and it was still the same two outcomes it was a minute ago...and the shooter was still fifty yards away not seeing him: walking, *Pop-pop-pop*...walking, *Pop-pop-pop*...walking, *Pop-pop-pop*....and suddenly Lucky's thoughts were clear, and the two outcomes both looked to be perfect, for different reasons. Lucky started running toward the shooter, seemingly halving the distance between him and the shooter with each stride, like a runaway roller-coaster descending from the upmost peak of the ride, never slowing down.

Which of the two outcomes is going to come of this? Lucky thought when he was just a few strides away, and the shooter still had not noticed or had faced him. One more stride and Lucky knew now it was too late for him to pivot, fire, and kill him. Like a movie in slow motion, which suddenly was too fast, Lucky was on him, lowering his head and burying his right shoulder as hard as he could into the shooter's *Guns for Nuns*, t-shirt, causing the semi-automatic weapon to fire randomly, almost apologetically, before becoming ejected from him, and onto the cement, the force from all of this ejecting the gun further away from them. This outcome was now decided, and now there was another thing which Lucky had not planned for. *What am I fighting for?* was Lucky's immediate thought, as he and the shooter began wrestling on the ground.

4
Standing Helplessly During The "Unthinkable"

Oh *fuck, where the hell did, he come from and what's in this for him?* was Peter's first thought, followed by, *How could I get tackled before I could get the Taylors? Maybe I did get them.* His next thought was about escape, but Lucky was large and solid, and Peter's struggles only brought him chest-to-chest with him. Lucky's chest and bulky flannel shirt pressed firmly against his *Guns for Nuns* lightweight tee. Over his left shoulder lay the gun, and Peter's struggling was less to get away from Lucky, more to be able to reach the gun; kill Lucky; and continue his onslaught. *This was not in my plan,* he thought, as sirens began to blare, and his life, the one he always knew. was over.

※ ※ ※

Peter was too tired to continue the struggle. Perhaps he could have played possum and then summoned all his strength, in a surprise move to push Lucky off him. At this point, it was desperation, but he didn't have enough strength to escape Lucky's grasp, which would invoke death by police. As the sirens grew louder, the commotion was now no longer at a distance, but directly above him.

There were sounds near and far of his demise, immediately of him being caught, and farther away, the sounds of those harmed. Suddenly, there was daylight as Lucky was removed from on top of him, but just as quickly, a replacement three bodies trapped him with their weight to the ground, handcuffs clicking onto his arms and his legs. When he was pulled up to kneeling position, the person who had first tackled and thwarted him was also by him, hands behind his back, just like he was, handcuffed, and looking almost as if they were both praying.

※ ※ ※

The Taylors, legs frozen in fear, managed to survive. So did Juliet Debrusk who also had been at the rally. All of them stood still, not running, not ducking—just standing there, each having moments of "not again," the trauma response initiated in all three of them for having lost loved ones. After their losses they had "what if I'd been there" moments that mentally kept both Candace and Ophelia alive, and then feeling completely helpless.

Now that they were here, feeling even more helpless, how they all wished they could never have "not again" moments ever again. Even the rest of the country got relief, growing tired of seeing it on the news. Instead of the complacency response initiated by television viewers, Matthew, Mary, and Juliet had powerlessness, and fear. Also crossing the mind of Matthew Taylor was the thought of wishing it had been him instead of his daughter, but now that there was a chance of it being him, he realized how much of a coward he was in both the options, as today's event played out. All of their quickened heartbeats and breath-holding slowed and returned to normal as they heard sirens and stopped hearing gunfire. Their legs could move and began walking, Juliet a few feet in front of the Taylors. The closest building was a bar. When Juliet Debrusk held the door, she couldn't place the familiar resemblance of Matthew and Mary, but they certainly recognized Juliet from the various research they had accomplished regarding the death of their daughter.

"Mrs. Debrusk?"

Juliet stared back, her forehead lines more distinct.

"We are the parents of Candace Malone," Mary said.

It took Juliet a few seconds to process, as the absence of music in a bar in Nashville seemed louder than a full band, the *pop-pop-pop* sounds of gunfire playing over and over in her head. Juliet's head suddenly cleared, realizing what Mary Taylor had said to her.

"We are all so sorry," she said awkwardly as she stepped in to give Mary Taylor a hug, the blood rushing from her face right before she lurched unbalanced, nearly unconscious, into Mary. Mary wasn't able to catch her, but her fall to the floor was slowed down, causing Juliet to slide gently down her torso. Mary's first reaction, from the way Juliet slowly fell, was that she had been a shot and needed medical attention. Mary's eyes moved quickly, searching for a t-shirt or a bar rag, as Juliet lay face-down on the ground. She turned her over immediately, looking for the wound, to see if there was any first aid she could offer, while still scanning for a cloth to stop the bleeding.

But there was no wound.

And there was no blood.

"Ophelia?" Juliet said, only seeing Mary's shadowy

figure bent over her, a response she would utter, searching for anything that could be Ophelia for the rest of her life.

5

The Reluctant Hero

Once upon a time, in a place close to your home, there was a hero who didn't want to be a hero. A handsome, rough-around-the-edges man was born to the media as a hero, the type of guy America needed to solve their inconvenient gun problem. The hero was a good guy with a gun, even though he wasn't carrying one at the time, but he had one in his car. If you are a good guy, in the right place, and at the right time, you will do the right thing. Even if it's not correct, it had the outcome that fit the narrative.

It doesn't matter if it was a shooter attempting to kill innocent people; the evil person could have a knife if America took his guns away. It's not the guns. He could have a car and run people over. He also might be a brick carrying man, whose only fault was that he was mentally ill and wanted to smash that brick into hundreds of innocent people's faces. If you are a good guy, you would prevent this, and you would be the main story on the television news. You would be the main story because why would they give attention to the shooter, the stabber, the driver, or the brick carrier and encourage more of those events? You are a good guy.

"Best to act modest," the director said to Lucky.

※ ※ ※

After Lucky was cleared and released, the local news and print newspapers contacted him, and, at first, he refused to talk to them. Everything was just too fresh. A few months later, after medication kept the voices out of his head, he agreed to appear on *60 Minutes*, for a million dollars, which the NRA agreed to match if they had say in the editing and approved the final product. It was like a win for everyone in America, the producer of *60 Minutes* was overheard saying.

Lucky's *60 Minutes* interview didn't get aired the way it occurred. Specifically, not aired in its entirety. Most of it was edited out. The parts where he said, "I was surprised to see him so close," and "Then I ran at him as fast as I could," and "The gun no longer was a factor," and "We wrestled for a bit," and "It was either him, me, or hundreds of other people," and "Then the police pulled me off," and "They didn't know who the shooter was," all aired.

What didn't air was "I was planning to kill myself, so I didn't care if I died," and "If it wasn't him, it would have been me," and "I heard voices in my head telling me to kill, but I left my gun in the car," and "He is exactly like all of us in some way, given a gun and an opportunity." Those were left out. The same producer again was overheard, this time saying, "I couldn't tell if we were interviewing the hero or the murderer." Later, the producer sold the unaired audio and video to *Rolling Stone*

Magazine for 1.5 million dollars.

Months later, *Rolling Stone Magazine* had a split photo for their cover story, Lucky on the left, Peter on the right, with the headline, "Meet The Reluctant Hero" which, besides the footage taken from Lucky, used interviews from Bobby-Joe Malone, Juliet Debrusk, Matthew and Mary Taylor, Kelly Granta, Grace O'Halloran, and Abby Shipp, who did her best to not say much to them. They even found the woman that yelled at Candace Malone in the restaurant, but that was an easy get because she was a social media darling before Candace's assassination disrupted her fame, as the news moved away from her onto the next thing—a couple of big shootings which occurred after Candace was gunned down. Grace was identified as the voice inside Lucky's head, but she didn't speak badly about Lucky in the story; neither did, for that matter, Abby, who didn't say much at all. Neither portrayed him as a bad guy, but didn't portray him as a 'good guy' either. Grace was surprised that Lucky had reached the level of distress that he had, and that her voice— her demanding, horrible voice was the one he mused to be influenced to do bad things. "I had no idea...just finding out about it now," she would say to everyone that contacted her after the article was published.

Kelly Granta provided some insight about mental health, but not the way the NRA would have wanted. In the article, noted as an expert on forensic psychological minds, Kelly Granta contributed more column inches about Lucky's mental health than Peter's, because she had taken a leave of absence immediately after Peter's assault by coffee cup, her concussion, and the brief hospitalization—it was still too traumatic for her. Kelly Granta covered almost everything except, *if you need help, call 1-800-273-8255*. Sometimes help can only do so much, but she gratefully was alive. She also was relieved that Peter Botchovich was not allowed by the State of Tennessee to contribute to the article, especially since she knew he'd have a lot to say.

Abby was tight-lipped during the interview, only saying that none of it surprised her after knowing Lucky and then hearing about Peter's history. "It just seemed that everything came together in a perfect moment," was her only quote. "After his dog died from his neglect, of course."

※ ※ ※

"I can't believe that this all happened," Graces voice once more filled Lucky's head, "and I had no idea!" Lucky, on the other end of the phone call, was surprised to hear her voice, as it had been missing from his head for a long time. The voice this time was not yelling or berating him, and Lucky was able to visualize the softness in her he remembered. Lucky didn't know if this phone call represented something good or something bad, something lucky, or something unlucky, but he was more than happy to be in the middle, as too much of his life had been consumed by good vs. bad, right vs. wrong, and conservative vs. liberal. It didn't matter anymore for him to be lucky or unlucky, he had to reach acceptance in what he did have control over.

"Let's not let it go this long before we talk again," she said.

"Yeah, I think that would be OK," Lucky agreed.

"You sound good," Grace said.

He paused for a bit, then said without any presumption or cockiness, "You know, for the first time in a long time, you do too."

Timothy Gager

Timothy Gager has published 20 books of fiction and poetry, which includes his latest novel, The Shadows of the Seen, forthcoming with Pierian Springs Press in 2025.

He hosted the successful Dire Literary Series in Cambridge, MA from 2001 to 2018, and started a weekly virtual series in 2020. He has had over 1000 works of fiction and poetry published, 18 nominations for the Pushcart Prize.

His work also has been nominated twice for a Massachusetts Book Award, The Best of the Web, The Best Small Fictions Anthology and has been read on National Public Radio. Please check-out his decade long well-known writer's interview and book reading video show:

DIRE LITERARY SERIES
on YouTube

Also by **Timothy Gager**

Fiction & Poetry

**Best of Timothy Gager,
Edited by Robin Stratton**
Anthology, 2023 Big Table Publishing

Joe the Salamander
Nove, 2022 Golden Antelope Press

2020 Poems
Poetry, 2021 Big Table Publishing

See Timothy's Complete
List of Published Works
via either of these websites:

HeatCityReview.com

PierianSpringsPress.com